8/10

Jason Berger

About the Author

Sean Ferrell's story "Building an Elephant" won the Fulton Prize from the *Adirondack Review.* His short stories have appeared in *Bossa Nova Ink*, *WORDS*, *Uber*, and the *Cafe Irreal*. *Numb* is his first novel. He lives with his family in Brooklyn, New York. You can visit him online at www.byseanferrell.com.

NO LONGER PROPERTY OF
SCHLOW CENTRE REGION LIBRARY

SCHLOW CENTRE REGION LIBRARY
211 S. Allen Street
State College, PA 16801

numb

numb

A NOVEL

SEAN FERRELL

NEW YORK • LONDON • TORONTO • SYDNEY • NEW DELHI • AUCKLAND

This book is a work of fiction. References to real people, events, establishments, organizations, or locales are intended only to provide a sense of authenticity, and are used fictitiously. All other characters, and all incidents and dialogue, are drawn from the author's imagination and are not to be construed as real.

NUMB. Copyright © 2010 by Sean Ferrell. All rights reserved. Printed in the United States of America. No part of this book may be used or reproduced in any manner whatsoever without written permission except in the case of brief quotations embodied in critical articles and reviews. For information address HarperCollins Publishers, 10 East 53rd Street, New York, NY 10022.

HarperCollins books may be purchased for educational, business, or sales promotional use. For information please write: Special Markets Department, HarperCollins Publishers, 10 East 53rd Street, New York, NY 10022.

FIRST EDITION

Library of Congress Cataloging-in-Publication Data

Ferrell, Sean.

Numb: a novel/Sean Ferrell.

p. cm.

ISBN 978-0-06-194650-9

1. Amnesiacs—Fiction. 2. Congenital insensitivity to pain—Fiction. 3. Identity (Psychology)—Fiction. I. Title.

PS3606.E756N86 2010

813'.6—dc22

2009038720

10 11 12 13 14 ID/RRD 10 9 8 7 6 5 4 3 2 1

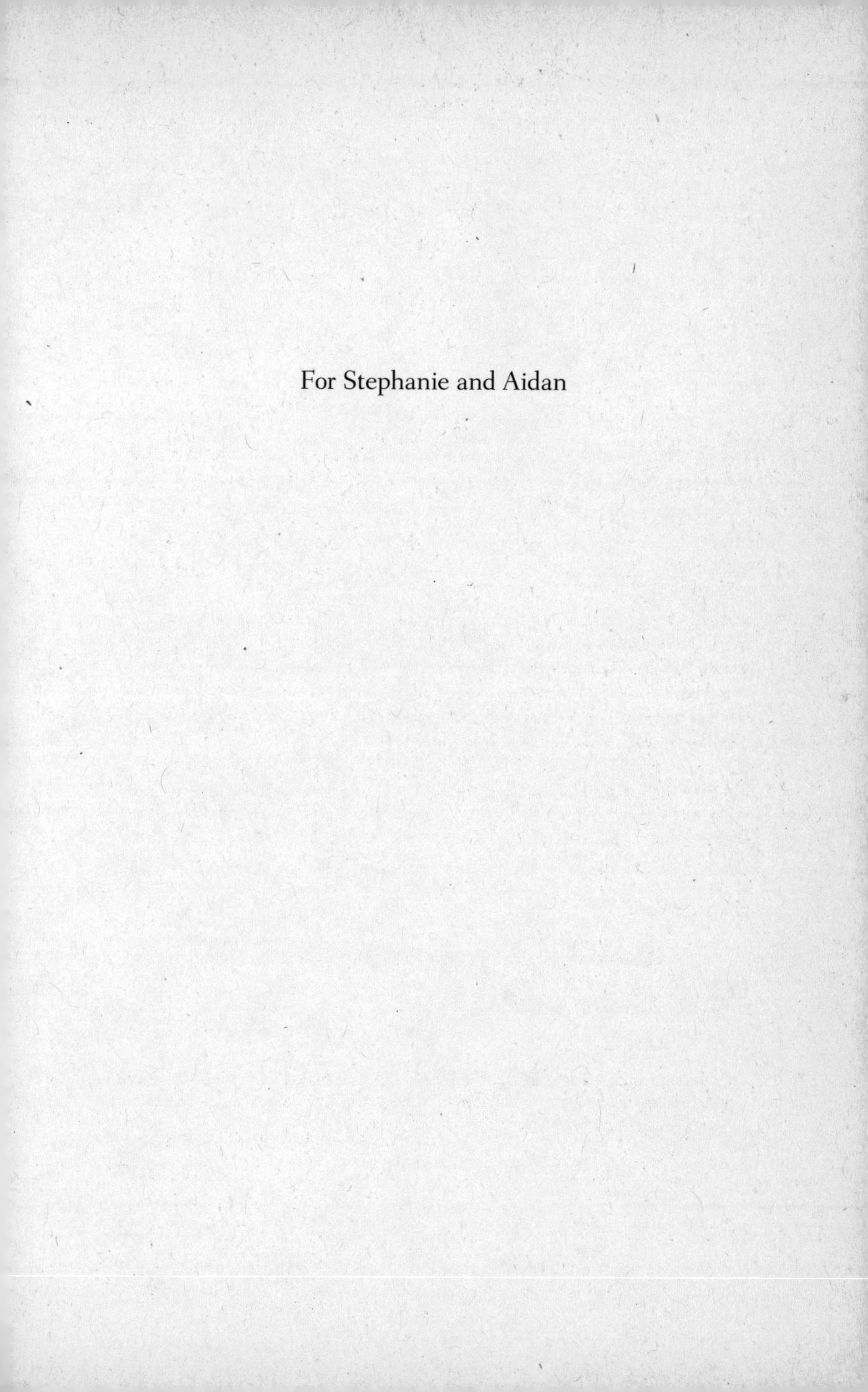

For Stephanie and Aidan

one

MAL RESEMBLED NOTHING else as much as a poorly gathered scarecrow. Over six feet tall, with kinky reddish blond hair and three days of beard, he wore a cheap plaid dress shirt, very old jeans, and no shoes or socks. A scar above his right eye showed where a juggled machete had ended an errant toss. His long arms seemed to grow out of his unbuttoned sleeves. As he lifted the television antenna over his head, his dark eyes glowering at the poor reception on the screen and his high cheekbones casting a skeletal shadow across his face, I thought he might be losing a battle with something unseen by anyone else but him.

I met Mal in Texas. He had a television in his trailer with a coat hanger duct-taped to the antenna. Two channels came in, both cloudy with static.

"Doesn't matter where you go anymore," Mal said while readjusting the hanger, bending it into a diamond shape. "With cable and satellite, the free antenna stuff is getting harder to find. I don't care what they say—digital antennae or not, they're cutting back on the signal. It's a ploy to make us buy new televisions from the corporations."

I didn't know what to say to that. I often didn't know what to say in response to Mal. He either left no option for debate or was spouting a conspiracy theory I couldn't comprehend.

Mal said, "You gonna take Tilly up on his offer?"

"I don't know."

"You know, doing your act is one thing, but this is a stupid bet."

I didn't know if it was stupid, but it was simple. Me and a lion in a cage together. If I did it, the circus would get a ton of cash. All for the enjoyment of a local oilman who thought my nail gun tricks were boring.

Mal said, "You know, pally, if you are gonna perform, make sure it's what you want, not what Tilly wants."

"I know." I thought I knew.

"You could just get your ass outta here. Go to New York or LA. Your act would fly there. Get on TV. Or movies."

"Maybe."

"Yeah, if only." He chewed on a piece of ice, cracked it between his teeth. I watched him as he chewed. It looked like shards of glass.

I hadn't always been in the circus.

Early one morning, after a sandstorm had ripped through north Texas, I wandered into Mr. Tilly's circus. I wore a black suit and blood ran down my face. As I stumbled around, I left a meandering trail in the fine dust that covered the ground, the sparse weeds, and the narrow, hard-packed dirt that passed for a road. The tops of the circus tents and trucks and trailers all sat like stones poking through the dirt, and I teetered between them. When some of the carnies came up to me, I said, "I'm numb."

This became my name.

I didn't know him yet, but Mal followed my tracks back out toward the highway. Everyone expected a car wreck, something new and fast wrapped around a telephone pole. There wasn't anything. My tracks just ended. Mal told me later that he was so freaked out to find nothing but a dead end, to see my footprints, perfectly formed and wandering east and west, come to a sudden, inexplicable end at the edge of the highway macadam, that he ran back to the circus with his heart in his throat.

My memory doesn't go back much further. It only barely has a grip on my wandering trip from the highway; beyond that, nothing.

Tilly didn't want a lawsuit, so he hired a doctor. One from a nearby town willing to drive out for a couple large bills and free tickets for his family. I had a bad cut across my scalp. My head was shaved to give me stitches. Tests were run. Only one thing seemed wrong: I didn't feel pain. Heat, pressure, and cold came through, but no pain. The doctor said the only disease that fit the symptoms was congenital insensitivity to pain with anhidrosis. I can't forget that word, *anhidrosis*, even though I have no idea what it means.

The doctor said, "It could be congenital, but you don't fit all the symptoms. For instance, you perspire. That makes this appear more psychosomatic." He faked a cough after the word *psychosomatic*. Other than that I was fine. "If that word can be used for someone who feels no pain," the doctor added. He tried to smile as I thanked him.

Everyone tried to smile at me as I waited to get over being "Numb" during my first weeks in Tilly's circus, but there was always a nervous hesitation. It was a simple sign that I didn't belong. I never got over it. No one knew who I was, and so they were less than interested in meeting me. Mr. Tilly gave me a job working with the roadies setting up and tearing down the circus tents. He felt bad for me. It was hard work, fast, and we never stayed anywhere long enough to do anything but the work. I hammered poles and tied off tent ropes. I mended holes in the impossibly old and weather-beaten canvas. I ate lunch in the shade of a truck or trailer and slept in one of the tents on a folding cot that was held together by duct tape and prayer. I hung around with Mal, who as a performer had a trailer, and tried to talk with Darla the Rubber Girl when I could.

I couldn't figure out what made Darla so appealing. When compared to images in magazines, Darla was a girl who might have been considered plain. Her hair was dirt brown and her eyes were a little too wide apart, but her smile and full lips drew most of the attention. That and her body's ability to contort itself into pretzel shapes. Strangely erotic pretzel shapes. Not that her act was what fascinated me. I was more interested in how she licked her lips when she was nervous or how she twisted her hair to let air get to her neck on hot days. Most of the roadies had a thing for her. She had the best of the ancient trailers, was always offered seats in the shade, and never got the dregs of the punch or powdered lemonade that was mixed up at the end of performances. Others spent their time backstage smoking or getting themselves mentally ready to stand on the stage and entertain the terminally bored. I spent my time watching Darla. If she was bothered by stares over the edges of coffee cups and awkward pauses in conversation, she was kind enough to not mention it.

One morning late in the fall, as we made our way south, we stopped outside a little town north of the Mexican border. Sandstorms and unpaid debts had been following us for weeks and made putting the show together nearly impossible. The wind whipped the tent flaps back and forth and the main tent looked like it was ready to lift off the ground.

Tilly ran around holding his filthy cowboy hat in place. He was trying to get us to unload the animals but the crew was lethargic. We'd spent three weeks heading farther south, selling tickets to the few people who showed up, and barely made any money. There was hardly enough to buy food, let alone pay wages. Tilly ran the circus on force of will. He didn't want it to stop, so it didn't. I wondered if everyone there was like me, had just sort of wandered in and been given a job.

I had just tied off a tent rope and one of the flaps was blowing so hard that it cracked like a whip. As he ran by, Tilly shouted to me to nail the flap back. I grabbed a nail gun from the pickup, held the canvas in place, and tried to shoot a nail through. In order to get the nail to really stick into the poles I had to press hard into the gun as I pulled the trigger. When I pulled the gun away I couldn't move my hand. I'd nailed myself to the pole.

I was embarrassed. The others already teased me about not knowing how to tie decent knots. Now I was stuck to a pole. I pulled my hand hard, but the nail was deep in the wood. The skin was purple and getting darker. I pulled at it more but thought the flesh would tear before the nail came out, so I stopped. I was surprised by how much stretch there was in skin.

I shouted to a couple of the guys nearby. No one heard me. Finally Mr. Tilly came back and I waved him over. "What is it?" he said. His faded hat had a small gray feather in the band, and as he leaned over me a huge wind gust came up; the feather blew out, circled around between us, and then tore away. We watched it disappear and he swore under his breath. When he looked back at me he swore again. In the pink of my hand was a black dot.

He said, "Is that a nail?"

"Yessir."

He looked at me and gave me the same sad smile the doctor had. "All right. We'll pry you loose."

He got a hammer from the roadies' truck. When he came back several of the roadies followed him. Mal, who earned a double paycheck by working on setup as well as performing as a fire-eating machete juggler, came too.

"You okay?" he asked. Unlike the others, he showed a little concern.

I said I was. They worked at getting the nail out and by the time they succeeded the whole circus was watching. Everyone but the animals stared. I'd been less embarrassed when I wandered into the circus covered with blood.

The hole in my hand cleaned up fine. I had a bruise around it the size of a quarter, but the hole itself was barely there. Tilly helped me wash it out. He looked at me quickly as he poured hydrogen peroxide on it, saying, "Let me know if this hurts." Then he shook his head as he remembered that it wouldn't. Not at all. As he closed up the mostly empty medical case he kept in his trailer he sat back and rested his head against the wall. Behind him was a black-and-white picture of a crowd of circus performers lined up. They all looked healthy and strong, their leotards clean and the animals powerful. At the center was Mr. Tilly, his hat new, with a handful of bright feathers in the band. His grin was wide and bright. He was a young man.

Tilly looked up at me, circles beneath his eyes. His hat rested on a table that doubled for eating and a desk. Papers and dirty dishes were layered on it. His trailer smelled of smoke, and, as he looked at me sadly, he pulled out a pipe and started to pack it. In my head I heard what he would say next. *You gotta go. I can't have someone nailing himself to my tent poles.* I waited for him to say this. I stood there, looking at him and his pipe, the yellowing picture on the wall behind him, and the hat with missing feathers on the table.

Smoke began to fill the trailer. He said, "Son, have you ever thought of getting into show business?"

I had not. One week later I was up on a stage with Mal, Darla, and the other freaks.

Describing the performances is like trying to describe what the nails feel like in my hands. There was a presence, a pressure, but I was always aware that I was missing part of the experience. Other performers had a look in their eye, a sort of hunger or thrill. A few of them, like Darla, even looked afraid as they prepared to go out. I stopped being aware of the audience. Mal said more than once that even though I lacked showmanship, I didn't need it. What I did sold itself.

When I first arrived at the circus the lineup was Rose

and Sally, Mal, Darla, and The It. Fat lady, skinny lady, fire-eater, sexy contortions, and strength. That was how Tilly described it. When I joined the show, I took The It's place as the finale. Tilly said that I combined fear and power, and fear was the best closer possible.

"Nothing sells a show better than fear. Scare them at the beginning and they'll keep watching. Scare them at the end and they'll come back."

The It was originally the main freak of the show. Tattoos wrapped around his eyes, great snakes that curled down his face toward his neck. From there they turned into tree branches and the branches grew along his shoulders and intertwined to form a trunk near his belly. The trunk disappeared into his waistband. When I first met him, he told me how much his tattoos hurt when he'd had them done. How many years it took. "I got so that I liked the pain," he said. "But you wouldn't know about that."

"If it hurt so much, why do it?" I asked.

With a sneer he said, "Because I'm an artist."

After I replaced him as the finale he refused to talk to me. Mal told me that The It went to Tilly and yelled that "some freak" wasn't going to take his place.

"You're not gonna let him say stuff like that, are you?" Mal said.

"I don't think there's anything I can do," I said. "Besides, I have to clean my hammer and nails off. The blood is caking on pretty thick."

I didn't know that my last performance in Tilly's circus was going to be my last. After the show, Tilly approached me about a challenge from a rich eccentric who owned some nearby oil fields. He wanted to see me put my "talents" up against the circus lion. I said I'd think about it. I went back to my trailer and sat quietly, doctored my newest wounds. A breeze blew through the trailer, found its way through gaps around the windows, cracks in the glass, and past the bent aluminum door. The trailer whistled from all the holes. A stack of bowls sat on the floor by my feet, ready to catch dripping water if it rained.

I washed the holes in my hands and feet with soap and alcohol and hydrogen peroxide and covered them in white cotton gauze and medical tape to hold it in place. I went through more medical supplies in a day than the circus had previously used in a week, yet Tilly never complained, despite the cost. These new wounds would heal in a day or two. I rubbed lotion over my shoulders to keep the scars from the audience-thrown darts from tightening up and stepped out for some air.

I heard performers and crew members in the main tent. There was laughter and conversation. I could tell they'd heard about the challenge made by the oilman. They buzzed about how much money it would bring to the circus. I stood outside the tent, listening to their excitement, my eyes on the misaligned stripes on the canvas, the result of a rushed repair job during a performance when a strong wind had ripped a ten-foot tear.

The roadies came back with food. Everyone lined up for dinner. It smelled like Mexican, which I hate, so I just wandered between the trailers.

Clouds rolled in from the north, heavy and low to the ground. The air below was dark and sharp tongues of lightning leaped underneath. Thunder rolled across the red-and-tan prairie.

"It's gonna be a big one." Darla leaned against the side of her trailer. Her blue sequined leotard hung from a coat hanger by the door, and in her door window hung a suncatcher. It was Garfield the cat, made from a wire frame and clear plastic, one of those children's toys you put the beads in and melt in the oven. Darla wore a bright red tube top and cutoff jeans. Somehow she made the rust on the side of her trailer seem as if it had been applied by an artist.

"It looks like it," I said.

She pushed some hair from her face and a breeze caught it and held it back for her. She smelled like salt and flowers. "If you do that thing that Mr. Tilly asked you to do, that would be great," she said.

"You think so?"

"Hell, yeah." She smiled. It felt as if she was confiding in me in some way. "You'd be saving us all a bunch of heartache. I mean, how long's it been since we saw a paycheck?"

I didn't say anything. It was hard for me to think of myself as saving anyone. I was doing this for reasons I couldn't figure out. If Darla became grateful, then all the better.

Darla looked north. The storm was moving toward us, rolling like the ocean. She reached out and took my hand.

"Want your palm read?"

"Sure."

"Oh." She'd noticed the bandage that wrapped around my hand, covered my palm. A spot of blood was growing in the center. She looked at it as though it was covered in shit.

"Don't worry about that." I pulled my hand away. "Maybe some other time."

"No, I'm sorry. It was just, you know. Let me see it again." She took my hand back and loosened the tape, undid the gauze. She pulled back the bloody cotton and stared intently at the hole that ran into the center of my hand. "Don't you ever hit anything important? Artery? Bone?"

"Not yet."

"My, my," she whispered. "You've got quite a love line under here." She smiled her secret smile again and winked. I stole a glance at her breasts in the tube top. "No wonder you keep it covered. You'll draw attention to it otherwise." I licked my lips and tried to look somewhere, anywhere else, but couldn't. "You've got to be careful, though. You've nicked it with that nail of yours. You'll end up breaking your heart that way."

Without warning she was kneeling on the ground at my feet. She looked up at me with a grin and said, "Come down here."

I knelt beside her and she lay down on the dirt in front of her trailer. Her right breast looked ready to sneak out of the tube top at any second.

"When I was a little girl," she said, "I used to do this when a storm came. Come on now, lie down." I laid next to her, our heads nearly touching, and looked straight up. Just above us was the still pale blue sky with the storm clouds sneaking in, and the edge of her trailer, with its little antenna for her TV and the sequined leotard hanging by the Garfield in the window. It was like a photo.

"My mother would yell at me when she found me doing this." Darla held my hand, her fingers on my palm, playing around the hole. "I grew up in tornado country. Kansas. She worried that I'd get sucked right up."

We lay there, watching the sky grow darker as the sun set, the edge of the storm overhead. It came quick, like a blanket pulled over us. The sky fell. Dark and heavy drops hit the ground around us, Darla squeezed my hand, I felt a shudder run up my arm.

"Here comes the storm," she said.

Rain poured down on us and in moments the dirt was wet. Not a dry spot but those under us. The rain on the trailer roof sounded like Mal's TV on a station full of static.

"It's so heavy it hurts," she said. I couldn't feel that, but I imagined I could so that we'd have that in common.

I ended up imagining not what the stinging rain might feel like to me but what it was doing to Darla. In my mind's eye I saw her from a great distance, lying in the dust, small black spots around her from the first drops, then I rushed toward her as gravity pulled me down and I pressed into her. I was the rain, in my vision. The feeling of her slippery skin was all I had in me as I lay there and held her hand. We looked at the clouds and rain, and the sequins of her costume sparkled in the dark gray above us.

"I'm heading in now, honey. I'll catch a cold if I stay out much more." She gave my hand a squeeze and sat up. The hair around her forehead was wet, and little dark fingers of it clung to her temples and cheeks.

I lay there in front of her trailer as she bounced up. The rough edges of her cutoffs dripped water as she stood in her doorway. The suncatcher clanged against the window. "Go in, silly," she said, her grin like Garfield's. Another secret. "And good luck."

In a wet haze I walked to the large-animal tent to look in on Caesar, the circus's one and only lion. If I did what Mr. Tilly had asked, the lion and I would soon be roommates.

The air in the tent was still and hot and smelled of shit and sawdust. Caesar's cage sat in the center of the tent and was as long as an eighteen-wheeler's trailer. Next to it rose the main tent pole. Rain leaked in near the top and ran down the side and pooled at the bottom.

Caesar panted in the stale, humid air, his sides shaking heavily, and as I stood there the air became thick with his breath.

I watched him. Water dripped off my nose and fingers. The dark fur of his mane hung around his head, feathered beneath his chin, and led to a trail down the belly. From beneath an exhausted brow, his golden eyes followed me. He had that distrustful and disinterested look that cats have, as if my leaving was the one thing that would bring him pleasure. The flesh on his ribs was loose. Like Mr. Tilly said, he looked old.

I don't know how long I stood there. Without a sound, Mal joined me. "He's not so tough." He swatted me on the shoulder, then shook water from his hand. "What the hell happened to you?"

"I was in the rain."

"No, I mean, you're bleeding. And covered in mud." He pulled at my shirt collar in the back. "There's a trail of blood back here." He lifted my shirt.

Yuri, the animal caretaker, watched us and smoked a cigarette. He was a Russian immigrant who had somehow come to the States with Caesar. In his coveralls he looked like a cadaver draped in cloth—there was no muscle on him, as if it had all dried up and fallen away. I wondered if Tilly was able to pay for both Yuri and Caesar to eat, and if Yuri might not have volunteered to give his portion to the cat. At his side he held the shovel he always carried. I didn't know if it was rust or not, but it always looked dipped in blood, blackish red at the tip.

Mal said, "You've got a piece of glass in your back." He pulled it out and showed it to me. A thumbnail-sized splinter of brown glass, probably from a beer bottle, was wet with my blood. He handed it to me and I ran my thumb over the edge.

I said, "It must have been in the dirt by Darla's trailer."

"What were you doing lying down by her trailer?"

"Watching the rain fall." My fingers kept playing with the shard, as if trying to forgive it for cutting me.

Mal watched me for a moment and then took the glass back. "I don't know what you're up to, but you're not gonna start making keepsakes out of the things that hurt you." I knew he wasn't only talking about the glass. He didn't like Darla and couldn't understand why I spent so much time trying to talk to her. But he didn't get rid of the glass then either. It needed to be kept, for a few moments at least.

I said, "What would you do, Mal? If Tilly had asked you to do this?"

Mal shrugged. "Don't know. Probably would do it. You know, because nobody else wants to."

"Does he look hungry to you?" I asked.

Mal looked at the cat. "No. A little tired, maybe." He squinted at Caesar, played with the piece of glass. My blood dried on his fingers. "Maybe a little done in by the heat."

Yuri came over to me and smiled. "You the dude who's going to rumble in the jungle?" he asked. His Russian accent was there, but barely. I told him I was. He eyed me up and down, then ordered me and Mal to step back.

"I have to open the cage, feed the lion."

Caesar knew what was going to happen. He stood and paced the cage's length, back and forth, his mouth open, the tip of his pink tongue visible.

"Look at how dull those teeth are," Mal said. He was right. They were dull. Then he added, "But they sure are big." We stood there a minute looking at the cat, then Mal said, "Do you think those teeth could break the skin, or would they just grind?"

I regretted checking in on Caesar.

Yuri pulled out a large plastic wagon. There was a pile of meat on it, fatty cuts of steak. "It's horse," he said as he unlocked the cage and used the shovel to push the wagon in. I could smell blood. It was the horse, I hoped, but it could have been the cut in my back, which was still bleeding. Suddenly young and dangerous, Caesar growled and leaped at the cage door. Just as he reached it, Yuri slammed it shut, then tapped the bars of the cage with the shovel. "You've got food there, kitty." He laughed and turned to us. "He would rather hunt for his food, you know." I could see it in Caesar's eyes. Caesar wanted something he could toy with. His disappointment with the wagon was obvious—his tail no longer cut the air, his ears fell back against his head—but still he stepped toward it and sniffed it gently.

As Mal and I turned to leave, Yuri called to me. "Hey," he shouted. "If you hurt my cat, I'll kill you." He held his shovel at his side. Behind him Caesar began to rip into the meat. Despite how dull his teeth looked, he had no trouble tearing pieces in half and then swallowing them with little, if any, chewing.

Mal tossed away the piece of glass. It sailed into the darkness, its energy somehow gone. From somewhere to our right a radio played music with someone singing in Spanish. The trailers, dark except for a few solitary, brilliant windows, wallowed before us. As we stepped away from the tent, our footsteps loud in the mud from the rainstorm, Mal cleared his throat.

"You'll want to clean out that cut," Mal said. "You don't want to get an infection before your big day." He said "big day" as if he were spitting the words out, as if they tasted wrong. Our paths took us to separate trailers and I heard his door slam shut after him as I climbed the steps to my own.

That night the cut on my back left blood on my sheet. I woke up stuck to it. It came free with a dry tearing sound, and the cut bled again. I climbed out of bed and tried to get ready for my noontime visit to Caesar's cage. The outfit Mr. Tilly wanted me to wear hung on my door: a Tarzan of the Jungle getup, one shoulder strap, bad leopard print, one piece. I wasn't about to wear it and started to pull on my jeans, but stopped. An occasion like this only happens once. I put on my suit, the one I'd arrived in. Out of some misplaced habit I ran my hands through the pockets, as if looking for keys or a wallet, a picture, anything. I'd never found anything there before, but on this search I found a business card that had slipped partway through a hole in the pocket lining. I pulled it out and saw that only one half was legible; the other half was black with dried blood. It was so soaked that it was now brittle and the card itself flaked. On the half I could read was part of a name and address:

*This article of clo*XXXXX
is the property XXXXXX
*Costumes, I*XXXXXXXXX
Located at 34XXXXXXXX
*New York, N*XXXXXXXXX

I read the card and put it away quickly, as if afraid somebody would see it. Hand in pocket, I rubbed it between my fingers. My heart raced and for several minutes, perhaps more, I forgot about Caesar, about my impending event, and I sat and listened to my fingers scrape against the card. I knew I might not have brought it with me. It could have been anyone's blood. I looked out the window and watched the shadows shift. The sun rose higher outside. I was going to be late. I pushed the card deeper into my pocket and stepped outside.

Drivers and a few roadies wandered around outside my trailer. I figured they were there to see me, so I tried to walk tall as I crossed the muddy compound. My shoes slapped across the wet ground, and I left a trail behind me in the thick muck. I was nearly to the tent when I slipped, almost fell in the mud, but caught myself on a tent flap. I swung for a moment and behind me someone yelled, "Hey, Tarzan!" I straightened my tie and went in.

Inside the tent it was hotter than the previous night. Murdoch, the oilman, was there with two men I hadn't seen before. One was a younger, better-dressed version of Murdoch. The other had a video camera and was taping everything around him: the cage, the lion, his feet for a moment, the top of the tent, me, my feet. At the speed he spun the camera around I thought that Murdoch would never be able to watch this again without getting nauseated, which was good. There was something pornographic in the idea of watching this again, I thought. I didn't want to be in porn.

"There he is, Sonny," said Murdoch. He grabbed the shoulder of his young look-alike and pointed at me. Sonny turned and stared me up and down, the same careful examination that Yuri had given me the night before. The cameraman filmed me. "That's the guy we're paying to wrestle the lion." He looked as if he'd just paid for a new car with a wad of stolen money.

Sonny, hands deep in his pockets, head lowered, said, "He don't look so tough." His voice was deep and he slurred his words together. "I've seen tougher."

"I'm sure you have," Murdoch said. "But still, he's getting in that cage and he's gonna wrestle that lion." He swore quietly to himself and said, "I'm so excited I could piss."

Caesar had his back to us. He panted heavily, his ragged ribs rising and falling in the thick air. At the side of the cage, Mr. Tilly grinned like a stupid child. He bounced up and down in place, which made his belly move from side to side. He said, "Are you set? Psyched?" He gave a thumbs-up and looked at the entrance, where people were coming in. "Look at them all," he said.

The stands were already filled. I'd never seen them full. Before this a good show had been twenty people. Outstanding was fifty. Over two hundred now filled the benches. At least a hundred more people stood wherever there was room. There were more children in the audience than I'd expected, sitting on laps, or up on shoulders so they could see over the crowd.

Tilly said, "You've got to be ready. Why aren't you wearing the outfit I left you?"

"It didn't fit," I lied. "Can I ask you something?" I walked around the cage and Tilly followed me. Watching for the cameraman so I wouldn't be overheard on tape, I said, "Is the lion drunk already?"

"No, but no worries. Look at him—he's exhausted. The heat is killing him and he barely slept at all."

The lion yawned. His teeth looked sharper in the daylight.

"What do you mean, no? You said he'd be drunk." He'd promised this the moment he suggested I take the bet.

"Well, he isn't. There have been people in here for hours; we didn't get a chance. Besides, I don't even know that you can get a cat drunk. Can you? Damned if I know." He talked rapidly, words linked in chains. His bounce intensified.

"Listen to me," Tilly said. We walked away from the cameraman, who had begun to follow. "You'll be like a superman facing down a savage beast. Damn, I wish that Tarzan getup had fit. That big kitten won't mess with you. He looks ready to drop dead from the heat. It's a hundred and fifteen in here. He'll never even touch you."

His eyes looked everywhere but at me. For the first time I saw Tilly's desperation. If people would pay to see me hurt, then he would hurt me, lion or no.

"I don't know why I'm doing this, Mr. Tilly."

He finally looked at me. "Hell, son. 'Cause you're an artist," he said. "All these people are here to see you because you're a performer. That's the way it works."

"I don't know about that."

Artistry in my act was debatable, but audience enjoyment wasn't. There was always shouting and clapping and a small amount of nausea and vomiting. Even that seemed a positive reaction to my act. But this, somehow, felt odd. It didn't matter to me if people saw this or not. If no one was there at all, would I do this? I began to think I might, if just to save the circus.

I was looking for Darla in the crowd when Mal grabbed my arm and pulled me outside. We walked back toward the trailers and stood between two of them, tried to stay in their shade. Heat reflected off the trailers and pushed over us in dry waves. Mal carried a brown paper bag and wore a heavy work suit like Yuri had worn the night before.

"What are you doing in that?" I asked.

"I've gotta stand by, be ready to pull that lion off you. But I don't have a nice suit like you." He opened the bag and pulled out a large bottle of whiskey. A bright orange price tag read SALE $9.99.

I said, "You shouldn't go in that cage. You'll get hurt."

He stared at me. "You're gonna fuckin' wrestle with the thing, so shut up." He handed me the bottle. "Have a drink."

"Where'd you get this?" I tilted the bottle back and a sweet acid taste poured over my tongue.

"Tilly had me run into town last night. It was for Caesar. But Wally Big Bucks showed up and we couldn't give it to him." He grabbed the bottle and took several large swallows. He coughed and said, "That's worse than the lighter fluid I use to spit fire." He passed the bottle back to me and said, "I think that if the big cat isn't getting any, we should drink it for him."

After my second gulp I said, "This is awful."

"I was buying for the cat, not you." He pointed at the label. "See, it has a bird on it. I thought that was a good sign."

There was a bird. A haggard black crow, drawn in

profile, with circles under its eye. It looked ready to drop dead.

"How is that a good sign?"

Mal shrugged. "Cats like birds, right? But birds can fly out of danger, so you're like a bird now. You just let him dance around you and you fly out of danger."

We spent a quiet half hour as we took turns choking down Caesar's whiskey. We finished, and Mal hurled the empty bottle over the nearest trailer. We heard it refuse to break with a solid thud on the other side.

I reached into my pocket, pulled out the business card, and handed it to Mal. He looked at it, turned it over, turned it back. He flicked the bloody edge and some of the crusted paper broke free. The corners were gone, rounded to a scabby softness.

Mal said, "What do you think this is?"

I took a deep breath through my mouth, felt whiskey vapors follow it back out. "I guess it could be something about who I was. I don't know. Maybe a way to find out."

"Maybe." He played with the card and handed it back. Then he asked, "What're you going to do with that cat?"

"I don't know."

"Why do it?"

"I owe Tilly, I guess. He saved me, took me in, gave me work and food. Maybe I can save his circus."

Mal shook his head and said, "And that card, you think it means something?"

"I guess."

Mal looked down at his feet. "You ought to spend more time thinking about who you are right now. Who you want to be, understand? Think about that." Sweat dripped off his nose. "Right now, why are you going into that cage?"

"I don't know." Again I wondered if Darla would be in the stands.

"You're full of shit. You know." He looked out over the field beyond the trailers. Brown grass refused to bend as the hot breeze pushed past it. It looked abrasive and rough, like it never had been and never would be green.

I said, "You know how The It talks about me? How he says that what I do has no drama? He says it isn't an act. He says that I'm a spectacle, not a performer."

Mal nodded. "So you think this is different?"

"I don't know."

"Is that why you're doing it?"

I shrugged.

"Whatever the reason, you better really be sure. Really think it over. And when you decide you want to do it, make sure you mean it. And if you decide you don't, run away and don't come back, or hide, or say fuck you very much to Tilly and Captain Moneybags. I'll go with you. We'll get to LA and make something happen there. Whatever. Just make sure you're doing it for a good reason. And if you think you have one, I'll be waiting for you there." He pointed at the tent opening. I could hear the crowd inside now. I had about fifteen minutes. "I'll be waiting for you to tell me your good reason. And if I'm not satisfied with it, I'll knock you out and call the whole thing off."

Mal walked to the tent. He spat as he walked away, a slight wobble noticeable in his carriage.

I wandered around the compound, searching for a reason to go into the lion's cage. When I got to Darla's door I tried to think of a good reason for being there. I knocked and heard a muffled answer.

"It's me," I said. I heard something again. "I can't hear you." I grabbed the handle and pulled. The whiskey and sun conspired against me; I lost my footing and fell backward. For a moment I propped myself up on the door, but then it broke off its hinges. I fell on my back, and the door spun as it tore free. I saw Darla's Garfield suncatcher coming at me and heard the crash.

I lay still for a second. After I pushed the door off me I sat up and felt blood run down my forehead. The suncatcher was bloody, and the window spiderweb-cracked. I wiped at my forehead, and tasted a whisper of blood in my mouth. I sat in sunlight, looking up into the dark hole where the door had been. I couldn't see into the trailer but heard Darla say, "He broke my fucking door." Then I heard The It say, "Retard." I crawled toward the doorway and looked in, found Darla in a bra and panties, small image of a snake in one hand and a wet yellow sponge in the other. It was The It's tattoo, a decal. The It sat in a vinyl-topped chair, in white boxers, his neck and chest free of any of his signature ink. They were all sitting on plastic sheets by the sink, still waiting to be applied.

"Hurry up," he said, "before the glue dries."

"He'll see."

"He's already seen. Now hurry up. Those are expensive."

As I squatted in the doorway, Darla pulled her eyes off me and put the snake on The It's face. She laid it against his skin, gave it a gentle push with the sponge. Darla put it right where it should be, where it had always been. I stood, shaking, and stepped into the trailer.

"What are you looking at, freak?" The It said. His eyes were brown. A bottle of contact lens solution sat near the sink behind him.

"They're fake," I said. I meant the tattoos, or his yellow eyes, or maybe all of him.

"He's afraid of needles," Darla explained. She pulled away the sponge. The snake's head curled beneath his eye and ended abruptly. There must have been a second fake tattoo that would continue the snake's body past his cheek and down his neck. Darla stood up, arched her back. Her panties had little flowers on them.

"Don't tell him that." The It smacked her thigh, a playful, touchy slap, with the back of his hand.

"Hey, asshole, he already saw me put one on, remember?" She threw the sponge in the sink. She looked at me through her long bangs. "What do you want, Numb? Why the hell did you break my door?"

The It grinned. "Don't you know? Today's the freak's big day. Came over for a good-luck kiss."

She handed me a paper towel and said, "You're bleeding." I pressed it to my head and the blood soaked in. She pushed by me, pressed into me for a moment to get through the door, and said, "You sure did a job on this thing." She stepped into the sunlight, and her white underwear caught the rays. I followed her out.

"Door was nearly busted off anyway," she said. "Let's hope Tilly uses some of that money you're getting for this show to get me a new one, right?"

I looked down at the door, the bloody Garfield.

From inside the trailer The It shouted, "Why don't you go do your thing and let us do ours?"

"Shut up," Darla yelled. She shook her head and stepped around the door. She looked up at me and said, "You can't tell anyone about his tattoos, you know. He'd be out of the show for sure. Our little secret, okay?" She covered her eyes with her hand, as if saluting.

With my hand pressing the towel to my forehead, I mumbled, "Why did he tell me he got used to the pain?"

"Because he's a performer. No one looks if you don't have an act, right?"

She turned and stepped back into the trailer. The moment she stepped out of the light she disappeared, and The It chuckled. I walked away, paper towel against my cut. I stepped on the door, window glass crunching beneath me, and then I retraced my path between the trailers, back to the main tent. There were clouds to the south, but hazy and weak. Nothing like the last storm.

Mal stood at the entrance. His eyes grew wide as I approached. I felt a resolve that I hadn't felt before and knew that he could sense it.

"What the fuck happened to your head?" I pulled the paper towel away but pieces stuck to my head like adhesive.

"I got cut."

"It looks like Garfield." The suncatcher's metal frame had cut into my forehead like a stamp. He examined the cat on my head. "Doesn't Darla have a Garfield suncatcher on her window?"

"Not anymore."

He stared at the wound. "That girl's gonna kill you. You get cut every time you talk to her."

"I'm going to do it, Mal."

"I need a reason." He wouldn't look at me, just the cut.

"Because I'm the only one who will."

"That's not a good reason."

"Who are you to decide that?"

Mal thought a moment. "I guess you're right. Fuck it. Let's go."

We entered the tent. Sonny pointed at me and said, "There's the freak now." The camera spun around.

Mal looked at me and then at my forehead. “It already stopped bleeding. You clot fast. That’s good.”

“Why?”

“In a few minutes you’ll be in a cage with a lion. I’d think you would want to clot.”

“That’s true.” It was a good thing. I began to wonder how I could use it to my advantage. “Good. I’m ready.”

A shout burst from the group of roadies by the door. “He’s ready.” Another voice shouted the same thing from outside. I could hear word being spread across our sorry little circus village. It suddenly struck me as bizarre that anyone would even be there but me and the lion. What did I need Mr. Tilly, the cameraman, or the trainer for? I didn’t even need Murdoch, Sonny, or the money. This seemed like the most natural thing to be doing, going into the lion’s cage. I was the freak who played with danger, the only one who would wrestle the big cat. This was who I was. I straightened my suit jacket.

“Open the cage up.” I rubbed my palms on the thighs of my pants.

“Wait,” Mal said. “What about a time limit?”

“Time limit?” Murdoch said, as if Mal had asked for a solid gold pocket watch.

“You don’t expect him to spend the rest of his life in that cage, do you?”

“It might be the rest of his life,” someone shouted. The crowd laughed.

Mal stood between me and Murdoch. "How long? Sixty seconds?"

"Too short. Five minutes."

"Unless the cat is on him. Then we pry him loose and he's out of there."

"Right."

"This ain't so tough," said Sonny.

"Open it up," I repeated. I looked at the dirt between me and the cage. An ant crawled by, several of its legs not working. It hobbled in an odd semicircle past my left foot.

Caesar sat on his haunches, panting. Everyone there formed a ring around the cage. I stood near the door. I looked over my shoulder and saw people wandering in from outside, the other circus hands, performers, some of the Mexicans who'd been hired as part-time help. Mr. Tilly looked ready to pop out of his suit.

"Mr. Tilly," I shouted, "I quit after this." Tilly simply nodded.

Yuri stood at the center with me. He looked proud and artificial in front of the camera—his hair plastered to his head, a part down the middle. Like a child, he smiled nervously at me, then looked back at the camera and said, as if he'd been rehearsing in front of a little mirror in his dirty trailer, "Are you ready, sir, for your trip into the lion's den?" Tilly had paid him $20 for that line.

I looked at the gray tent, the pole, the heavy flies

buzzing around me. Yuri's eyes danced back and forth between Mr. Tilly and Caesar. Mr. Tilly smiled and nodded, then waved with the back of his hand, mouthing, "Go on, go on." He was a fat, bad mime.

I looked at Yuri and said, "Just open it up."

Yuri, his big moment about to be over, smiled and bowed to the camera and unlocked the door. It swung back just wide enough for me to step in and then, just that quickly, I was in Caesar's cage. Thirty feet long and ten wide, probably illegal for a cat his size. Everything outside dropped away. Caesar at one end, me at the other. He stood, turned in the cramped end, and swayed back and forth. His eyes didn't leave me. I felt like his little red meat wagon.

I heard heavy breathing, my own. Caesar and I couldn't break eye contact. Muscles twitched along his ribs and flanks. Jesus Christ, he was big. What was I thinking, calling him old and skinny? He was the king of the jungle, for God's sake. The cat stopped swaying and stared straight at me.

He took a step forward.

"Holy crap!" someone shouted. I realized that I had stepped forward too. The cat took two more steps, and so did I. Our eyes were still locked. We were connected. He'd hypnotized me, or me him. Either way, I sensed our destiny in that cage, that long walk to each other, straight ahead. We reflected each other. At heart I was the big cat and he was the skinny amnesiac. No option but straight ahead. I took a step and he did too. He panted heavily through his mouth; his tongue lapped at his nose, then hung limp. He started a deep moan that grew to a roar, a yell, nothing like in the movies. I put my arms out at my sides and shouted back.

"I'll meet you halfway," I yelled. I felt sick from the whiskey.

We moved closer. Only ten feet separated us. His growl grew to a purr.

"Here, kitty kitty . . ." I whispered. I suddenly remembered a nursery rhyme:

Algy met a bear.
A bear met Algy.
The bear was bulgy.
The bulge was Algy.

I was glad it wasn't about a lion.

Caesar stood before me, head low, tongue nearly to the ground. A horrible growl erupted from him. The muscles in his toes clenched, claws digging into the wood beneath him, tendons tightening as his legs tensed. He fell onto his haunches, back arched. He bellowed and began to vomit on the floor. The reek of bile and blood washed over me. Chunks of half-digested meat and fat poured out of him and spread across the wood, over my shoes. Caesar gulped air, strings of saliva and foam hanging from his mouth. Then he collapsed forward.

I stepped back, slipped, and fell on my ass. Caesar, startled, batted me with one paw, his claws hooking immediately into my thigh, but he couldn't manage any more, not even a growl. With closed eyes he rested in the mess he had made.

Pandemonium swept through the audience. Screams and shouts tore the air. People ran for the exits, others toward the cage. The spaces between the bars became solid as faces and bodies pressed up against them, practically trying to get into the cage with Caesar and me.

"I'm stuck," I said to the crowd. "He's got his claws in my leg. I can't get them out."

Mal and Yuri stood next to the door. Mal grabbed Yuri and pointed to the tent flap. "Get a vet."

An hour later a vet showed up in a tuxedo and white leather sneakers. He wore a plastic boutonniere and his breath smelled of toothpaste. Mr. Tilly ran in with him.

When Mal saw him, he said, "Who was getting married?"

"My daughter," said the vet.

The crowd pressed in harder around the cage. They'd grown quiet except for those complaining about not being able to see, or those claiming that they were being crushed against the bars.

Mr. Tilly grimaced as he watched the vet take in the scene through the bars of the cage. Before him lay Caesar, half-open eyes rolling back and forth, and me with the lion's claws deep in my thigh. The vet turned pale and said, "Holy Jesus." He walked to the wrong part of the cage and had to be led to the cage doorway.

The vet rubbed sweat from his forehead. "How did this happen?"

Mr. Tilly said, "He went in to feed him." He had stayed on the other side of the cage. His eyes darted between me and the vet. The vet approached and knelt beside Caesar's head. He talked to him gently.

The vet, his eyes dark and wet, said, "I think he's dying." Then he looked at the claws in my leg. "You came into the cage to feed him? Why would you come into the cage?"

"I was here to wrestle him."

"No he wasn't, no he wasn't." Tilly shook a fist, like a villain in a silent movie. "Why would you say that?"

The vet didn't pay any attention to Tilly. "Wrestle? Was he drugged?"

"No," Mal said. "But he was supposed to be drunk."

It took a moment for this information to sink into the vet's head. Finally he said, "What a bunch of assholes." Caesar growled in agreement and tried to open his eyes. "Why the hell would you do this to an animal?" The vet knelt in vomit without concern. "I'd like to know where you get off."

"We've got it on tape, if you would like to see." I smiled weakly, feeling like the asshole he thought I was.

They set about removing the lion's claws from me. Caesar lay there, eyes rolling and vomit and blood caked around his mane. Tilly held the lion's paw, and the handler, his eyes full of tears, plucked the four claws from my thigh. The jagged cuts bled, and, as Mal pulled me away from the lion, Darla approached. She glowed, lit from behind by sunlight through a gap in the tent flaps.

"My God," she said. "God God God." She helped me stand and Mal ducked under my arm. As I limped out of the cage the crowd applauded.

"Why are they clapping?" I asked neither of them in particular.

Mal looked at me, mouth turned down. "Are you kidding?"

Darla followed us as we dragged my leg back outside, then said to Mal, "Take him to my trailer so I can patch him up."

In her trailer Darla had pictures from magazines cut out and stuck to the ceiling with masking tape. Irregular rips of tape held the pictures. Men and women smiled down at me. They threw knowing, meaningful looks over their shoulders and shimmered with their own beauty. They were all dressed better than the three of us.

Darla slapped my uncut leg. "Hold still, dammit." She knelt before me with a needle and thread, straddling my ankle. She'd sewn up two of the cuts and had two to go. The green thread crossed back and forth evenly across the wounds, pulling them shut.

Mal leaned against the bathroom door. "Where'd you learn to do that, Darla?"

"I was in nursing school once."

"No shit." He leaned over her, looking down at my leg, then gave me a thumbs-up and a wink. "Lookin' good."

"Get outta my light," Darla ordered.

"I'm outta here. Gonna go check on the big cat." As he stepped to the door, he smiled at me and gave a nod toward Darla, his grin wide. He propped the door up against the side of the trailer as he left. I wondered how I would pay to have it fixed.

She poured hydrogen peroxide over the cuts again. She had used a whole bottle of rubbing alcohol already. White foam bubbled over my leg. For a long time, perhaps from the first time I'd seen her, I had wanted to spend time with Darla. Now here I was, alone with her in her trailer, with my pants undone and bunched around my ankles. The eight-inch lacerations were unexpected, as were the sewing-thread stitches, but I would take what I could get.

She looked up at me. "You don't feel that at all, do you."

"No." I cleared my throat, tried to think of something to say. "So, you were a nurse."

"I don't like to talk about that," she said without looking up. The needle jerked through my skin, the torn edge pulling back and away as she ran the thread through it. I looked into the red of my leg. It was like a landscape. White bubbles of peroxide glistened like clouds.

"Sorry about your door."

"You already apologized."

Desperate for something to say, I looked around the bed. She watched my eyes. She said, "I know. I got a lot of pictures." She smiled.

"You sure do." The pictures covered every inch of wall around the bed, across both sides. Without thinking I asked, "Doesn't The It mind them all?"

The needle stopped, then tugged again slowly. It felt like Morse code in my skin.

She didn't say anything. I closed my eyes and thought about the afternoon rainstorm and how close I'd been to her lying on the ground.

She concentrated on the wound. As it closed up, the red growing smaller—a seam in me—I felt her pulling away. By the time she snipped the thread I still hadn't thought of anything to say, to cover my tracks and take me back to a minute before. I felt like a boulder that had smashed through her roof and now someone had to come and break me into a million pieces to take me away, bit by irregular bit. She stood and dropped the thread onto her table.

"I think that will heal up okay. We'll take those threads out in a week. Keep it clean."

I looked down at the green lines that crisscrossed

the lion's claw marks. I reached to the floor, grabbed my pants, and pulled them up as I stood.

"Thanks," I said.

She didn't say anything until I got to the door.

"Get some rest," she said.

As I walked away I felt tugging, as if Darla still held the threads in my leg.

I slept for a few hours. I got up and the sun had just set. The stars had begun to appear and the only light from the trailers was the blue flickering of televisions. I walked to the main tent and found Mr. Tilly talking with the vet. Turned out that old Caesar was of an endangered breed: a Barbary lion. He would be taken away from the circus and given to a preserve somewhere in Florida. The vet had arranged it.

Tilly saw me limping at the entrance and yelled, "What the hell you doing up? Rest that leg before it falls off." I hadn't seen him angry before. His face reminded me of Caesar's before he vomited.

I walked back out into the trailer area and got turned around. I found myself standing between two trailers that hadn't been near each other earlier. There would be no reason to move them around, I thought, and I leaned against one to get my bearings. Nearby a fence separated us from another field and, looking at the sporadic growth on the other side, I realized where I stood. I had wandered into the empty spot where Darla's trailer had been. She was gone.

The It left with her. He'd probably fled because I knew he was a fake, and Darla had left with him because what else could she do? Certainly not stay and stitch up holes in my body as I slowly pinned myself to the circus and drained out a trail of blood as it limped toward its sad end.

two

"THIS WAS SUPPOSED to be my night off," I said to myself.

Mal spun the claw hammer around his fingers like a cowboy pistol trick. "Hey, if you aren't enjoying this, why watch?" I was unsure whether he aimed this remark at me or the guy vomiting into his book bag. Mal brought the hammer down and the second nail went through the delicate stretch of skin between my pinkie and ring finger. He almost drove the nail flush to the surface of the bar, and I wondered how difficult it would be to get out.

The man vomiting had bet Mal that I couldn't take a nail through my hand without screaming. He sat on a bar stool with his back against the bar. Sweat ran off his nose and he might have been crying, though it could have been the strain of puking. I'd grown accustomed to this sort of reaction to my act. Some fell ill, no matter how much they wanted to see me get pierced.

"I guess you are numb," he said. He clutched his bag to his lap. Small black spots of my blood peppered it.

Redbach, the bartender, said, "Do you think so?" His gut stuck out the bottom of his shirt, which read ASK ME HOW I FEEL. He pulled at his sideburns, one of his annoying nervous habits—along with an eye twitch and laughing at inappropriate moments—and laughed. He pointed at the bar and the guy laid down everything he had in his wallet. Eighty-seven dollars. Then he stood and started to leave.

Mal called after him, "Hey, don't forget to come see the show. Numb here has a staple gun trick that will make you piss." The guy didn't look back. He walked out onto Avenue B and into a windy New York City night.

"And tell your friends," Redbach added. I barely knew Redbach. He tried too hard to be my friend. He was the type of person who would suggest jumping off a bridge but be the last to leap off himself. On the other hand, Mal had always backed me, or so I kept telling myself, based on his willingness to stand by me in the Caesar incident, his "quit Tilly's circus" camaraderie, and his steadfast support as we struggled up the East Coast to New York, all because of a strange slip of paper I'd found in my pocket connecting my suit to an East Side costume shop. I already had a following in the city in the freak show crowd because of him, his efforts to sell my act, to hawk for me at every bar and impromptu sidewalk show. His own act held no crowds—New York apparently had no appetite for fire-eating.

After the vomiter left, Mal told Redbach he should go out on the street and charge people to come in and see me nailed to the bar. Redbach hit the door and started calling out to a small crowd at the corner.

"I'm not in the mood," I said. "Pull these out." I looked at my right hand. The flat tops of the aluminum nails poked out the back, just above the meat between the thumb and forefinger and next to the pinkie, and purple indentations surrounded the punctures. An ashtray on the bar almost touched my ring finger. It stank. I pushed it away with my free hand.

Mal tapped the hammer on a bar stool and pretended not to hear me.

"Pull them out," I said.

He wouldn't look at me. "We can make some extra cash."

Outside, Redbach shouted, "Come see the man who can't feel pain. He's nailed to the bar, right inside. This is not a trick. Watch as nails are stuck into his hands and feet. Maybe drive one in yourself."

If I could have pulled myself away from the bar, I would have walked out. "Who the hell does he think he is, saying that?" Redbach's dive bar didn't get any business, no matter the night or desperation of passersby. The only reason he made any money now was because

Mal suggested our little one-man freak show would be a draw and Redbach agreed. We, meaning I, had performed three times in nine days. The first performance had been for an audience of four. The second for twenty. A line jostled out the door on the third night. This was supposed to be a night off. The holes in my hand from the last show, close to these new ones, hadn't closed up entirely and they began to bleed a little.

"I want to go back to our shitty little hotel room and clean these out," I said.

I'd started this night just hanging out in our hotel room, a two-bed room at the St. Mark's Hotel. There must have been a sale on glossy school-bus yellow because that was the color of the recently painted room. Paint fumes and mildew smells from the bathroom drove me to wander the hallways. I struggled to make the Coke machine stop stealing my quarters. When the heavy blond woman behind the bulletproof glass tapped the handwritten sign that read NO ALCOHOL IN THE HALLWAY, it was time for me to get back to the room. I wasn't drinking alcohol, but I didn't argue.

In the room I hadn't known what to do with myself, so I ended up just staring at our little black-and-white TV with the speaker-wire antenna that ended with a coat hanger wrapped in aluminum foil and taped to the only window in the place. This TV had followed us ever since we ran away from the circus and headed north from Texas. Over three weeks we had hitchhiked and made rest-stop bets for rides in the back of eighteen-wheelers. Whenever we stopped Mal would hook up the TV and find a channel with reception. "Someday we'll be on TV," he'd say. When we finally reached New York City, we did street performances to scrape together the money for a week in the shit hotel we were in. And since then, for almost two weeks, I'd been driving nails into Redbach's bar with sad regularity and looking through the Yellow Pages for the clothing rental store that might be the source of the business card. I'd visited a dozen during the days and called more in the evenings. None used cards like I'd found. That night I called a few more until I realized the hour, too late for any of them to be open. I couldn't concentrate on TV, and the paint fumes were dizzying, so I'd wandered over to Redbach's under the deranged theory that I could go in and just have a drink.

When I'd arrived, I'd found Mal talking with Redbach and a guy with a huge green knapsack. He laughed, his arms swinging. I heard Mal say, "It's gonna be amazing. Nobody has ever done anything like this." Then he saw me and his eyes darkened. Before I sat down Mal told me the guy with the knapsack didn't believe I could do what I could do. The betting had started, and now I was nailed down again.

"Listen," Mal said. "We showed that loudmouth, and you're here—"

"I'm always here. All we ever do is sit in this place."

"I mean, as long as you're already nailed down, why not?"

"You started this. That guy was just having a drink, and you started all this. Now get me off this bar."

"He said you looked like a pussy."

"You asked him if I looked like I'd ever been nailed to a bar. What was he supposed to say?" My arm tingled, probably due to a nail against an artery or vein. My legs creaked. I could hear voices outside bartering prices with Redbach. People would be coming in any second. In the mirror on the other side of the bar I saw myself, a skinny blond white guy without enough to eat and too little sleep, nailed to the bar. I wore the Batman tee one of the roadies had given me before I'd left the circus. Mal had been given the complementary shirt, red, with Robin's *R* in a black circle over the right breast. As far as I knew, he'd never worn it. His dreadlocks, unwashed and uncontrolled, danced with his reflection in the mirror behind Redbach's bar, the hammer wagging in his hands. If I looked tired, he looked exhausted. Until then, I hadn't noticed how out of it Mal looked.

People started coming in, and Mal said, "What the fuck are you gonna do? Call tuxedo places all night? Shut up and enjoy the free booze."

He took on the role of carnival barker, a ghastly imitation of Mr. Tilly.

"Come on in. You want to see the man who feels no pain? You might not have read about him in the papers, you might not have seen his picture in the magazines, but you can be sure you will someday. Don't ask for his autograph, though. He's pretty nailed down at the moment."

I hissed at him through my teeth. "I'm not in the mood, damn it."

Mal shot me a smile and said, "That's your problem, isn't it?" The floorboards groaned as more people stepped into the bar.

A woman with a crew cut and a lip ring asked, "Does it hurt?"

I looked up at the TV that hung over the bar. It received the same shit reception as the set in our hotel room. It had the fuzzing in and out of faces so you couldn't see any details, and I thought that it might as well have been a show about me because it displayed everything I felt. Unfocused, unclear, uncertain. I drifted back to Texas and an overheated trailer as I waited to go onstage, and a spiel Mr. Tilly had written for my act over a year ago leaked out of me.

"None of this hurts. I can't feel a thing. No one knows why. Maybe it's all in my head, or maybe it's in yours. I don't know. All I know is, it's hard to scratch your nose with your hand nailed down."

I always thought it silly, but when I started performing in the circus, Mr. Tilly said I needed a way to introduce myself to the audience. I'd been saying it twice a day, three times on Saturdays, ever since.

The woman with the lip ring snorted and inspected

my hand. "Fantastic," she whispered. "I want to buy you a drink."

Mal stepped behind the bar and poured me a whiskey. I took the drink and said, "Fifteen minutes is all you get," then I poured the shot down my throat.

People took turns walking up to examine the nails in my hand. Some of them pulled out cell phones and began to call people to get them to come see me, or snapped photos or videos.

"I don't know the name of the fucking place," said one man into his phone. Across the back of his head a tattoo read KAMIKAZE. "Just get the fuck over here. You'll freak."

People bought me drinks, and after ten minutes I was sweating alcohol. Too distracted by the redhead with the low-cut shirt and scratch marks between her breasts who pressed into me as she leaned over my hand, petting it softly around the nailheads, I didn't know how long Mal argued with the skinny guy near the end of the bar. The redhead cooed over my hand. This was another typical reaction to me. I'd seen people light up like they'd never been so moved when they saw me take a nail in the hand, or a staple in my back or thigh; people smiled in a way that said they hadn't smiled in years. Women like this one found it reassuring, I guess, like I somehow understood them or had been through what they had.

I realized that Mal and the guy were arguing about me. Mal's eyes, flickering between lazy and disturbed, begged for it to get out of hand. He had a hint of a bored smile. He often mistook boredom for "passion for drama."

"What you are saying, pal, is such bullshit," Mal said.

"This is a scam and you know it. This guy's just got piercings in his hands, and you've got everyone thinking this is some shit. I want my fucking ten back now."

"No, you don't. You want to give me another fifty and put a nail in my friend yourself, don't you." Mal handed the guy a nail and then turned to me and said, "Put your left hand up there, all right?"

"No." I said, "I want to leave."

Mal leaned across the bar, grabbed my left ear, and pulled it to his lips. "Listen," he said. "I could give you a hundred and one reasons why you should do this. Because you can. Because they want you to. Because they have paid for it. But I'm not going to waste my time. Put your fucking hand on the bar or I won't pull these nails out and you'll have to rip them out of your goddamned hand yourself, you shit."

Where had this guy come from? I wondered. He couldn't be the same person I'd come up the coast with. Definitely not the same guy who'd protected me in Texas, who'd demanded a reason for me to go into a lion's cage. His eyes were dark and he fidgeted with the hammer like it was hot. He smelled like whatever kept backwashing out of our tub.

I tried to step back but could only reach as far as my nailed-down arm would allow. Mal returned my glare. He looked down for a moment, then said, "Listen, man. We've been too fucking poor for too long. Let's just take their money, all right?"

My pulse drummed in my ears. I felt like a child who, despite being right, was ignored. My friend, my supposed protector, was using me for his own gain, trying to convince me it was for me and ignoring my complaints. For a moment I imagined that I had the nerve and the strength to pull hard enough to rip the nails out of the wood or to pull my hands free, tear the nailheads through my skin. I knew it wouldn't hurt, but there was still a part of me that understood some level of self-preservation. As the idea came to me I became weak and gave in. As always, Mal ran the show.

The crowd watched. A breathy, salty smell rolled off them. With one hand Mal held out the hammer to the skinny guy, and with the other he took a wad of crumpled bills. As Mal placed a nail against the skin of my left hand between the forefinger and middle finger, the guy raised the hammer above his head. If he had had anything to drink, I couldn't tell. He brought the hammer down in one perfect blow and drove the nail through my hand and into the bar.

The redhead held my glass for me and I took a sip of my drink, then she sipped it, like we were taking communion. Nailed down tight, my fingertips and palms began to focus on the rough grain of the bar. I couldn't move my hands, so I soaked up what little of the wood bar I touched, like a sponge, and, as I did so, I could read my fortune in it, like a palm reading in reverse. I saw my future: I was out of this bar tonight, and I would never be back.

The crowd around us watched quietly. The room must have had sixty people inside. The sweat and stale beer odors hung on to us all, and traffic noise blared in from the street. Outside, Redbach shouted for passersby to pay to see the freak inside. Mal pulled another nail, clenched it between his lips, and took out a third. The second was driven between my forefinger and thumb. Quickly, and with one sure shot of the hammer, he put the last through between the pinkie and ring finger. Little pools of blood seeped out along the bar and mixed with the beads of condensation falling from my glass.

I didn't respond. I never did. Mal, with a look, or Darla or The It or Tilly, any of them, with a simple glance, could make me sit and stay, like a trained dog. All the while, they drove metal through me and made people pay to watch.

"Like a butterfly in a collection," Mal said as he poured two drinks for us. Someone made a comment about me being a freak. "No. I saw him on TV," someone else said. Mal smiled broadly at me.

"Someone saw you on TV?" he said. "Must be the tape that oilman made."

Again, I focused on the old mirror behind the bar, some antique from some other place, a better place, with the slightest ripples running across its surface, ornate wood carvings of flowers and birds twisted, almost gruesomely, into one another across the top. And except for the nailheads poking up over my hand, each a little crooked and at its own angle, my reflection looked like that of a man simply resting his hands on the bar. Just a guy with a drink and a friend with a hammer. I watched everything in reverse in the warped mirror and wished for a moment that I could switch places with the calm stranger, the rested man with the quiet face and easy manner.

A woman with a long mullet dyed like a skunk's tail fanned her boyfriend with her handbag. He looked ready to keel over. The redhead jockeyed for position at my side as another dozen people walked in, trying to see past the crowd. More people threw money on the bar to buy me a drink. Everything had just the hint of a warp to it. The mirror distorted those further away more than those closer, and Mal, right next to it, reflected without flaw. He stood tall, king of the warped world. But then I noticed one small distortion in his reflection, at his center, near his heart, where a curl in the glass created a pinch in his body, made a small piece of him disappear as if it never existed.

Mal held the hammer over his head and said, "One hundred dollars and you can drive a nail into my friend."

Eyes lit up in the reflection; people raised their money and lined up to pay for their chance. Onlookers clapped. I looked at the redhead next to me, and she leaned in close and smiled. I could smell the sweat and rum coming off her.

I said, "They don't care if I can feel it or not. They just want to see someone hammer nails into someone else." She laughed as if I were joking and wrapped her hands around my waist.

From the back a guy in a Yankees cap yelled out to ask if we took credit cards.

By the time they were done with me Mal had over a thousand dollars and I was nailed, both hands and feet, in place. Still outside, Redbach was charging twenty dollars a head. Drinks poured themselves. Mal lifted a glass to my lips and tipped it into me.

"We better go soon," I said. "I'm bleeding here. I gotta lie down."

"You barely bleed at all."

"Yeah, but I've been drinking too. The only thing keeping me from falling down is that I'm nailed to the bar." I shook my head. "I'm tired. Pull these nails out of my feet. I want to sit down." My lips felt too large.

I had no idea what time it was, other than late. Mal started prying nails out of the floor with the claw of the hammer. He was finally listening. The alcohol must have sedated him because he hummed and he grinned at me as he worked at the nail next to my right small toe.

"You've gone soft. When we were in the circus, you could take your liquor."

I didn't say anything.

"What are you so quiet for?" he asked.

Once, back in Texas, a few weeks before running away from the circus, before the challenge to go into the cage with Caesar had even been made, I had been near the end of my set when a woman in the audience turned to the man next to her and said, "I can't believe he's so quiet up there as he's doing all that to himself."

The man had nodded and replied, "Yeah, well, you know it's the quiet ones you got to look out for. They eventually snap and then—boom!"

A few people had chuckled at the man's remark. I'd been snagged by it, stuck in midmotion as I prepared to ask for a volunteer from the audience to use the staple gun on my back. But when I heard that comment, whether meant as a joke or not, I simply stopped and turned and walked off the stage. At that moment I knew I should leave the circus. I didn't know that Mal would go with me, or where I'd go, or that a few weeks later I'd be in Caesar's cage, but I had a vision of myself, belongings tied up in a blanket and thrown over a chain-link fence as I ran across dry fields toward slow-moving freight trains. I knew I'd run away from the circus.

In Redbach's bar these memories rushed back to me as I watched Mal. I stood quietly, thinking of the fortune I had read in the wood. My days of allowing Mal to boss me around were over. I didn't know what I'd do. I didn't know what grand plan I should have. I wanted to sit down. I was tired. I could barely move my right ankle when he finally got my foot free. Disgusted, I realized I'd been standing barefoot in puddles of beer.

Mal said, "Listen, you had fun tonight. Admit it." He got the last of the nails out of my left foot and poured alcohol on my feet. "You don't even bleed. Look at that."

He was right. I moved my feet and couldn't find any wet blood. Just a touch of red dried at the holes where the nails had driven into the floor.

"Just pull these out of my hands."

Mal stood and rested the hammer on the bar. "Not until you tell me you had fun tonight."

"This isn't funny, Mal."

"Say it."

I chewed on the inside of my cheek and took in a deep breath. Someone had moved the ashtray back in front of me, right between my hands, and now I had no way of moving it. It stank, nearly as bad as I'm sure I did. I saw myself as if from above: small, and sad, and stuck like a roach in a trap, same as Mal; he just didn't know it. Actually, he did know it. He just didn't care. Or, worse, he was glad of it.

I said, "I'm sick of being in this shithole. I'm tired of these people coming in and staring." I was exhausted, more than I'd ever been. I closed my eyes and readied myself for

Mal's reaction, for his defense of the indefensible. Then I said, "And I'm sick of you telling me what to do."

It didn't come. I counted to twenty, and it still didn't come. I opened my eyes. Mal, quiet, ground his teeth, stared at me. I felt afraid and certain that Mal would do something to me. I could see it in the casual way he turned away, and as he looked over the dirty glasses and ran his hand across the edge of the bar, I thought he would turn and take the hammer and make me hurt. I didn't feel pain, but he would try to make me. Then he did turn toward me, but his eyes dulled over and a smell rose up around us, salty and coppery. Blood. I could practically taste it. I looked down at my hands, spotted only little drips where the nails first broke through the skin. Mal reached for the hammer on the bar and that's when I saw the cut. On the back of his hand, from his thumb to just past his wrist, a mouthlike gash opened at me. Blood came out and ran into a pool on the bar. It collected in the gutter and mixed with spilled beer and alcohol. It ran away from me.

I yelled for Redbach. Commotion outside, but no sign of him.

"What the hell?" Mal said. "I must have hit myself with the hammer." His eyes swam. "It's not fair. You get hardware put into you and nothing. Me, I bleed all to hell from just . . . You know, it does look like you've got holes in your hands and feet." Mal was drunk and distracted and apparently happy to bleed on me. "From where you drive the nails in. That asshole earlier was partly right. It's like you just have permanent piercings. You probably wouldn't even feel the nails if you could feel pain." Blood continued to run off his fingertips.

"Just get my hand free," I said. He pulled the nails from my right hand, his blood dripping onto my hands and the wooden bar, then gave me the hammer. My left hand was stuck to the bar in a little pool of beer and daiquiri mix. I pulled the nails out of myself, something that had become second nature to me, like shaving. There is a sucking sound when nails come out of skin. It's the skin trying to close up and keep you from bleeding to death.

Mal looked into the opening on his hand and said, "Look at this. You don't even bleed. Me, I'm a gusher."

I grabbed a towel from the bar and wrapped it around Mal's hand. On our way out people wanted my autograph and Mal told them to go fuck themselves. One guy in a leather jacket wanted to punch me in the gut as hard as he could. Mal called him an asshole and said I wasn't Harry fucking Houdini, who'd died after an unexpected blow to the stomach. Redbach asked me if we'd be back the next night.

We got into a cab without answering. The driver turned and smiled and I told him to get us to the nearest hospital. He looked at me like I'd just told the punch line to a bad joke.

"Hospital?" he asked, his accent thick. His hair was

cut like Elvis Presley's, and he wore sunglasses even though it was probably three in the morning.

"Emergency room," I said, pointing at Mal's hand. "Doctor." I pantomimed a sewing motion. The driver turned away slowly, kept looking at me in the mirror, and pulled away from the curb. The heavy traffic surprised me, and we moved almost immediately behind a bus, too close to its ad for malt liquor.

"I could use some of that." Mal leaned heavily on the door, the bloody towel tight against his hand.

Our cab followed the bus to the corner, then made a couple of rights. I watched the stragglers on the sidewalks, the last people who were wandering home. Some couples, but mostly people by themselves. There were young women with bags hanging from their shoulders. They walked past groups of men on street corners. All these men, from the ones dressed in expensive Italian shoes and shirts going home from the clubs to those looking through garbage cans, had the same look in their eyes as the women passed. Mal had that look tonight, I thought.

I turned to him and asked, "What the hell happened in there?"

Eyes closed and head back against the seat he said, "I cut my hand. What happened to you?"

The meter clicked upward. I said, "I can't keep doing these crappy gigs. I can't keep living in that shitty hotel."

"Do whatever you want," Mal said. "It was a mistake coming here."

For an instant I thought he meant the bar and was going to agree, but when he refused to look at me I knew he meant something else. I didn't say anything and after a moment, sensing I needed to hear more, he continued. "I never should have come with you to New York. It's gonna kill me. Should have gone to LA like I wanted, but you had to follow that fucking business card. You're gonna move on. You're fine. You fit in anywhere. Not me. I'm still in the circus, only it ain't in Texas. It's right here, being your babysitter."

I couldn't see. I was drunk and angry, and either or both blinded me. I hoped the cabbie might accidentally drive us into the river or headlong into a light pole. I heard my teeth grind. I said, "I never asked you to do anything for me."

His head bounced against the seat, his eyes still closed. "Didn't you? Would you even be here if I hadn't brought you? You'd still be in Texas. Probably still shoveling shit for Tilly, looking at that bloody card and saying, 'What do you think it is, Mal? Do you think I might have rented the suit there?' Couldn't get past the card. Couldn't get past Darla. If you'd listened to me and just paid that karma back on some other girl, you'd be fine. Instead . . ." He trailed off.

Car horns blared as we pulled up to the entrance of St. Vincent's Hospital. Mal paid the cabbie with money from the nail-driving show. Blood on the bills hid dead men's faces. Mine or his, who could tell? He handed the rest of the cash to me.

We walked around the waiting area, bathed in a mix of ammonia and mildew odors. The ceiling radiated wall-to-wall fluorescent lights and the air-conditioning vents blew a racket of cool air through the room. It wasn't a hot night, and the cold air that poured over us raised goose bumps on my arms. Right by the door a man lay facedown on a gurney, a white sheet concealing whatever poked from his back. A woman leaning against the wall wore a T-shirt that said HERE WE GO AGAIN. The seating area was full, but no one looked sick. An old woman knitted while watching over two sleeping children, and farther down a group of men in green coveralls huddled around one another, whispering, bunkering themselves from the rest of the silent room. It looked like a crowd waiting for a bus, not a doctor. From another room someone cried out. One of the men in coveralls hung up a cell phone in a panic, but he didn't get up.

Mal kept walking around the main desk. It sat in the center of the room, like a giant donut. Near the desk a TV hung from the ceiling. Mal pointed at it. "Look at that. I think that's you." It was me. A home movie of me made back in Texas. The show must have been one of those send-us-your-tapes-and-we'll-air-it-and-won't-pay-you-a-dime programs. We stood there, staring up at me in front of a lion's cage, until a man in scrubs approached and looked us up and down.

"What happened here?" he asked. He showed no surprise or amazement, no curiosity. He looked at a magazine he carried with him, folded back on itself and then in half, pinched to a clipboard as if to trick people into thinking he held only official medical documents.

Mal pulled open the blood-soaked towel and showed the doctor his cut. "I slipped while shaving," he said, "and my friend was recently nailed to a bar and needs to be disinfected. He's had his shots."

The doctor looked at the cut, then at me, then at my feet. "You're bleeding on my floor."

I looked down. I'd left my shoes and socks at the bar. Bloody footprints on the tiled floor wandered in lazy circles around the donut in the middle and were punctuated with drips from both my hands.

"Well," Mal said, "look at that. You do bleed."

I looked at the young doctor and asked where we should go. "With all these people here. You've got to wait your turn." Then he turned and walked away, reading his magazine.

We walked across the waiting area and found two seats that had opened up. I kept looking back at the TV, but it had gone to commercials. Mal unwrapped and retightened the towel on his hand. I watched as the blood on my hands and feet slowly dried.

"I don't remember ever bleeding like this before," I

said. I was a little scared. I didn't know if this meant something had happened to me. How many nail holes could a person have before it was too many?

Mal coughed into his hand. "I'm moving out when we leave here."

I looked at him and didn't say anything. I didn't know what to say.

"No," he said. "Forget that. You move out. I need that shitty little room. You'll make big money in no time. I've got no place else to go."

"Fine," I said, and then I made my way across the room. My stomach growled and I felt slightly dizzy. I hadn't had much to eat all day. I headed toward a table with coffee and cookies. On the TV my image popped back up, out of focus and shaking, about to perform the trick that drove me out of Texas.

My friendship with Mal ended just that quickly. He'd gone from being a guardian in Texas to abusing me in New York and now he'd kicked me out in an effort to get away from my success—if you could call being on a late-night video show success—angry that we'd headed east rather than west. I didn't know where to go or what to do. I was hungry and there was food on the table in front of me. As I continued to it I bumped into the young doctor, only now he had a mop and a bucket. Revealed as not a doctor but the janitor, more concerned with the cleanliness of the floor than the suffering of those on it, he slapped water to tiles.

"Hey, asshole," he said. "Quit walking around. You keep bleeding on my floor." He pulled the mop after me as I walked across the room, all the way to the cookies, and smeared my bloody footprints with his dirty gray water that smelled like black cherry soda.

three

FOR A VERY brief moment after Mal kicked me out of our hotel room, I thought I would end up living on the streets. The idea didn't scare me. The street just presented itself, without any other options around it. I left Mal at the hospital and took a cab to the hotel. On the way back it occurred to me that I held the money from my unexpected performance, so when I got to the hotel I stopped at the front desk to get a room of my own. I wondered if I'd ever had a room of my own.

The thin woman behind the glass, with her ringed eyes and beakish nose, looked like a strange, denuded bird on display. I thought she would never leave her cage, and it looked rarely cleaned. She asked if I wanted the room for the night or just for an hour.

"The night," I said.

"Wait, you're one of the guys in room seven, right?" She pulled out a piece of torn paper, a corner from a tabloid. "You got a phone call here while you was out." She slipped the paper under the half-circle hole in the glass and on it I found, written in the neatest hand I'd ever seen, a simple, telegram-style message:

Michael. Agent.
Saw show. Must talk.
Please call.

The Manhattan phone number at the bottom looked important; somehow the digits all made sense together. I memorized them without trying.

Mal was right. I'd have little trouble finding money, an agent, or attention for doing what came naturally to me: inserting sharp and jagged objects into my skin.

The next morning I called the number to talk to Michael. Instead I talked to his enthusiastic assistant, Robert. Robert took my call as a great sign. He'd seen my "show" live and gotten my number from Redbach.

"I know Michael will be happy you called." Robert spoke in a professionally manic voice. "You know, I showed him the tape. Even though it was, like, a copy of a copy of a copy, it was still pretty good. Michael agreed. We both thought you just have to have an agent." He sounded like a prophet revealing the mysteries of life.

"Great." I fought an urge to hang up. "Thanks."

Michael's office was in Times Square. The woman

behind the desk, who under any other circumstance would have crossed the street to avoid my type, warmed to me as if I had diamonds falling from my pockets.

Alternating mirrors and movie and television posters lined the waiting room walls. I glanced around. My face flashed by in the mirrors. I sat down and buried my face in an issue of *People*.

When Robert came to get me he led me down a hall lined with more mirrors and posters. Only then did I realize how bad I looked. I had worn my suit because I really didn't have any other clothes. Mal had lent me most of my other outfits. Now I was myself: crumpled, dirty. And the tear in the right pants leg from Caesar's claws hadn't repaired well.

"I'm so glad you called us." Robert flashed smiles at me over his shoulder, a beacon as we wandered through a maze of halls to Michael's office. "You know, I showed Michael the tape, and he loved it. He was shocked to find out you didn't have an agent." He said this as if he hadn't told me the exact same thing when we spoke on the phone.

"Yeah. By the way, did you have to pay Redbach for my number?"

"Well, he made us buy the tape before he'd tell us."

I asked what they'd seen on the tape. I had imagined it was me in Caesar's cage. I was wrong.

"It's you nailed to his bar. He sells them for twenty-five dollars."

"I didn't know there was a tape of that."

"You mean there are other tapes?"

"Yeah, well, it could have been the one of me in a lion's cage."

Saying that brought the reaction people normally save for watching me pierce nails through my hands. Robert stopped short and a man in a much better suit than mine stood in a doorway, eyebrows arched and mouth gaping. Their excitement made me nervous. They looked at each other a moment, then Robert smiled and said, "Michael, this is him."

Michael smiled back at Robert. It was some sort of infection. "Let's go into my office."

A window aimed up Broadway dominated the room. It was actually three windows that formed a slight arc, and the crowds on the street below flowed like a tide. The room felt like the bridge of a great ship plowing through the people. I imagined the building moving forward, the masses being left behind.

Michael and I sat in chairs facing the windows. We looked at each other over a small table with ice water pitchers and crackers. Robert brought a couple cups of coffee, then disappeared.

Michael reclined heavily into his chair, almost as if pushing back in order to tip it. His suit remained neat, even while sitting, and the sunlight coming through the window caught highlights in his slick hair. He treated the view as something he'd seen too many times for too many days. A distraction. Me he watched. It wasn't a gawk or a stare, which I normally received. Just an appraisal. I grew very aware of scabs and scars littering the skin between my fingers and thumbs. The staple holes along my neck and in my earlobes. The cuts on my lips from biting myself. The nicks on my face and neck from my razor. I could be so clumsy even while standing still. Even the cuts and punctures down my back and buttocks felt revealed. He took it all in, a judge of how I'd treated myself.

He remained silent.

"I'm not sure why I'm here," I said.

He grinned. "That's okay. I do."

Another minute went by in silence and the chair no longer seemed as comfortable. Michael noticed my fidgeting and poured me a glass of water. "Most people would want to pitch you this or that," he said. "I just want to tell you a story. You want to hear a story?"

"Sure."

"It's your story, actually. But I don't think you know it as I do. You know your story one way, just as you lived it. But I know it as it's presented right now, in one shot, just from the way you sit there, looking around and nervously jiggling your knees. I know it as the image of you as you are right now."

He stood and removed his jacket, placed it on a hanger on the back of his door, retook his seat.

"You're not really certain of where you've come from

or how you got here. Everything is a bit overwhelming, scary even. You're uncertain of whom can be trusted because you've been deceived in the past. But through all this uncertainty and deception, and sometimes good times, but often hard, you've had one thing, a gift, a talent that you have that no one else seems to have."

Michael stopped to turn one of the cups of coffee into a mess. He slopped too much cream and sugar into it. Tan liquid spilled over the cup's rim and settled into the saucer. He stirred at it as if beating it back and then laid the spoon on the table. A trickle of coffee trailed from the spoon's underside.

He lifted the cup to his lips, one hand positioned underneath to catch drips that would have landed in his lap. Before setting the cup back in the saucer he pulled three paper napkins from the serving tray. He lay them in the saucer, then placed the cup on top. He cleaned the spilled coffee from both cup and saucer. He lifted the cup and removed the napkins. He wiped the spoon and stray drops. He placed the cup in its saucer and the spoon to the side on a napkin, then threw the ball of used napkins in a wastebasket in the corner. He leaned back in his chair, and I examined the perfect still life he'd created out of his cup of coffee. The mess made just moments before gone, Michael returned his gaze to me. He'd obliterated disorder. *This is what Michael does,* I thought. *He takes the mess away and makes things neat and organized.*

"As I was saying," he continued, "you've never done

more with your talent than a quick display here and there. Few people have seen it, but when they do they are impressed. Despite this, you don't seem able to get anywhere. You feel like you're skimming along the surface. You don't know if you know what's happening. You don't know if you can trust people because you've been let down."

I was sure it hadn't been so warm when I'd come in. "Could I have some water?"

Michael nodded at the glass he'd already poured for me. "I know how hard it is to hear your own story from a stranger. How do I know all this? Because it's every artist's story."

"Artist?"

"Sure. Why not? You have a canvas; it just happens to be your skin. I can see the marks of your work on your hands and neck." Michael pointed at the window. "See the crowds out there? They don't know they need you yet, because we haven't made them need you. We'll carve them up into two camps, those who hate you and those who love you. When they argue about you, you'll be more than just a guy with pins in his skin. You'll be your own work of art."

I said, "I'll be a commodity."

Michael followed my eyes. "Exactly." He drank the rest of his coffee.

As I sipped my ice water I spotted something floating along the bottom. Something black and hard and crusty.

"You haven't even asked me where I'm from. About my past or who I was working with in the video."

"That's because nobody cares. It's not important."

"It's not?"

"Of course not." He went to a cabinet in the wall and opened it, revealing shelves filled with cameras, carefully laid out files and pictures, and a column of drawers running up to the ceiling, each neatly labeled. He removed a packet of film from one and loaded a Polaroid camera. "You want to tell your story. I'll help you tell it. Show me your biggest scar."

For an instant I thought about leaving. Then I felt myself scratching at my right leg through the stitched-up pants. Maybe there is something about wounds that makes them want to be seen; the ones Caesar gave me itched.

Michael mistook my delay for embarrassment. "Trust me." He locked the door. "No one sees this picture if you don't want them to, but when I take it you'll see what is important about your story and what isn't. You'll see who you can be."

I unbuckled my belt and lowered my pants. I showed him the scar that ran along my thigh.

"Oh, God. That's big," he said. "Hold still." He took a picture. I expected him to take more, to use up all the film from different angles and then create a file filled with my scars. Instead he took just the one, then turned back to the shelves. He put the camera back into its proper place, shut the cabinet, and fanned himself lazily with the picture, waiting for it to reveal my image.

He said, "There's something you're hiding from me. What you are afraid to say to me is the stuff you want to keep for yourself and that's fine. Don't tell me, don't tell anyone. If you share too much, it will start to haunt you. We're painting a picture of you. It can look any way we want it to."

The room quieted a moment, and the view of the street continued to plow along. Michael stopped flapping the photo and said, "I understand you've been trying to locate a shop that may be the place your suit is from. How's that going?"

"How do you know that?"

A shrug. "That guy selling the tapes sells more than just tapes. How goes the search?"

"Not good."

Michael smiled. "I didn't think so. You look lost. But you don't have to be. Leave what information you have with Robert and we'll get somebody on it. In the meantime, I want you to understand we can make you as big as you want to be."

"You make it sound easy."

"It is." Michael looked at the picture. "This is the picture of you that we're painting for the public. I think it's a pretty amazing picture." He handed it to me.

Instead of a picture of my thigh, focusing on the scar, I saw a picture of me. All of me. I looked confused and tired, my pants dangling around my knees, my eyes focused up and to the left, toward the window that you couldn't see in the picture. The light from outside illuminated me, and my hands hung at my sides. I must have been about to say something, though I couldn't remember what, because I looked ready to speak. I was sweaty and shiny and something in my face made me think of Mal. I felt tired and scared.

I said, "You're always looking for new talent, right?"

"Of course."

"Well, I have a friend. He's got a great act, breathing fire and juggling. He could use an agent too."

Michael nodded. He avoided eye contact. "I could talk to him, see his act. I'd have to see what he can do before I could agree."

"Sure. But if you were my agent and he wanted to meet with you—"

With a great smile Michael said, "My door is always open for my clients' friends." He took the photo back and said, "This picture is just the first that will be taken of you. Are you ready to start helping me show you to the public?"

I said I was. I pulled my pants up and buckled my belt.

four

MICHAEL INTRODUCED ME to Hiko, a tall, slender, blind Japanese woman with large eyes, long fingers, and straight black hair she wore up on top of her head. She had a beauty mark on her upper lip exactly where Marilyn Monroe had one. Michael told me never to tell her that. "If you never trust me about anything else, you should trust me on that."

"Why wouldn't she want to be compared to Marilyn Monroe?" I asked. "Monroe was beautiful."

"Someone told her that," he said. "She went apeshit."

Michael had been my agent for six weeks. I hadn't gotten any work yet, but he'd put me in a hotel, the Thomas, a semiupscale retro hotel in Midtown. I'd been there, on his tab, since signing the contracts in his office. At the time he told me, "You look like hell. Get some rest, let me take care of you." I tried to let him.

Michael also represented Hiko and had convinced her to do a portrait of me in time for an article about her in *Modern Art*. "You're so unique that chances are good they'd use photos of any piece based on you in the article. Great cross promo."

"She agreed to this?" She didn't know me; neither did the magazine, for that matter.

"First, she trusts me to do right by her. And that's what I do, for her, for all my clients. I'm very busy doing right by my clients. Second, it wouldn't be you in the article, it would be her art. But when she does you, it will be fantastic."

Michael had also warned me that she was blind. I asked Michael, "If she's blind, how can she do portraits?"

"You'll see. And, when she's done your portrait, it will get you work. Just watch. Hiko's too hot right now."

Michael drove me into Brooklyn for my introduction to her. He picked me up at the hotel in a black BMW.

When we got to Hiko's she answered the door, smiled shyly, and said, "I'm so happy to finally meet you." I believed her. She grasped my arm. Michael patted my shoulder and said, "I'll be out here. Got some calls to make." He walked back to his car, cell phone already speed-dialing.

Hiko held my hand as she took me down a dark hallway and into a kitchenette. No lights were on. Sunlight struggled to reach us through half-open windows far down the hall. She drifted ahead and pulled out a chair for me. Her head tilted like that of a small bird, and her long fingers moved gently, sensitive, I imagined, to every soft movement of the air. I was not uncomfortable, but afraid to disturb her. As if I might scare her off.

She turned to face me. "Have a seat."

She asked if I would like some tea. After I said yes she remembered she had none. "How about some chocolate milk?" she asked.

I said, "Sure," even though I don't like chocolate milk.

She poured us each a glass and then repeated her invitation to sit. I quietly obeyed.

She felt her way from cupboard to cupboard. We sat on mismatched kitchen chairs in the center of a room so small it only had a center. Both chairs were splattered with handprints of orange, blue, yellow. Like scabs on the vinyl. Paint and clumps of plaster covered the floor in splotches, footprints tracked back and forth. Her feet were long and slender, and her tracks were slightly pigeon-toed. Her pinkie toes didn't quite touch the floor when she walked.

"Michael thinks you're going to be a huge star," she said.

"Really?"

She sipped her chocolate milk. "You don't seem interested."

I didn't know how I felt. "I guess it's just so new."

"Has Michael taken you to any photo shoots yet?"

I said, "Just a Polaroid in his office."

"From what he says, that will just be the first." She was so dainty, I wondered if she actually took any milk in her tiny sips.

Sunlight came through the window behind her. Shadows broke through and scampered up the walls as Michael walked back and forth outside. With the kitchenette below ground level, I was able to look out the window at his legs. He was still on his cell phone.

Hiko turned an ear toward the window. "Is that Michael I hear?"

"Yeah. He's waiting outside." I kept watch on the curve of her lip and the small dot above it. "I think he's on his cell phone. I hate cell phones," I said. "They make people act so important."

"I disagree." She put down her glass and smiled, bowing her head as though embarrassed. "I think they are wonderful. They equalize everyone. When else would the wealthy walk around sharing one side of a conversation with strangers just like a schizophrenic? Next time you are on the street, pay attention to the conversations going on. People reveal remarkable details about themselves." She finished her glass. I hadn't started mine.

She said, "Now, let's get started." She reached out

to me. "Give me your hands." Her eyes gazed above me, as if to read a thought balloon above my head, and I couldn't help but blush.

Hiko wrapped her fingers around my hands and squeezed them. "Make fists," she said, and when I did she let go of my left hand and played both her hands over my right. Her fingernails scratched delicate lines on the back of my hand and circled the smooth purple blossom-shaped scars that freckled the skin between my fingers.

She said, "I want you to tell me when I am touching a scar." She started at my pinkie, and as she crossed over the gap between pinkie and ring finger I said, "Now."

"How many? Just one?"

"I don't know. Definitely more than one."

She felt farther, past the ring finger toward my middle finger, and I said, "There too."

She made a soft, thoughtful whisper and I said, "You know, I have scars between each of my fingers. And my toes. And some other parts of my body."

She opened up my fist and squeezed the skin between my thumb and finger. "It's so soft." She stroked it quietly. "It feels like a flower," she said. Outside, Michael laughed, presumably into his phone.

She ran her hands up my arm, stopping occasionally when she met a bump or ridge. "Are all of these scars from performing?"

"No." I blushed again. "I can be a little clumsy."

She laughed. "You're joking. How could you trust that you won't really hurt yourself?"

"I don't know. I don't think about it."

She reached up to my face. "If this makes you uncomfortable, let me know." She pressed her fingers against my chin, my cheeks, up my temples, and across my forehead. "You have some lines up here," she said. "An old scar?"

"Yeah. That's nearly gone. You can barely see it."

"What's it from?"

"A door fell on me."

She smiled. Her eyes moved around me but rarely rested on me. Sometimes they went through me. Michael had told me that our first session would be for introductions. When Hiko said that I should come back the next day, I wasn't surprised. I was surprised, though, when she said, "I hope you don't mind working nude."

"For the portrait?"

She laughed. "Yes, for the portrait. I do all my work as nudes."

I assumed she meant only I would be nude.

I WENT BACK the next day at midafternoon. The clouds of the previous day had turned to a thunderstorm overnight and the streets in her neighborhood smelled steam-cleaned. There were still puddles along the curbs and under cars. I found Hiko on her front stoop. She looked as if she were staring across the street and it didn't occur to me that I might startle her when I stopped.

She must have heard my footsteps halt because she tilted her head, and her sightless eyes shifted. "Hello?" Her voice was strong, but just underneath hid a quiver.

"It's me," I said. "I didn't mean to scare you."

For a moment she didn't say anything, and I imagined she ran through a list of denials, but finally she said, "Only a little." Her voice and smile were both soft.

She stood and followed the handrail down into her doorway. She knew just when to duck her head where a low-hanging pipe drooped above the entrance.

She showed me a back room where examples of her work covered a wall. They hung in sturdy frames; she called them "three-dimensional paintings." Most of them were gray and covered with massive amounts of detail and texture. There were faces, some body parts, and many abstracts.

"You can see I don't concern myself with color." Some of the sculpture-paintings were thick clay; others had paint. Some were layers of many colors, scraped with a knife. Others were just one or two tones. Blue-green. Canary yellow. Or gray, or white. Color was mostly an accident of material, of white plaster or gray clay, though sometimes it appeared as if she'd added dyes to the mix.

"I either have someone pick out the color for me or do it at random. I don't worry about it because I think color is arbitrary anyway."

I said, "They're beautiful."

She stood in the hallway, her head to one side, her large black eyes locked on nothing. She thanked me and followed the wall into her workroom. She took off her jacket and sandals and said I should strip down as far as I felt comfortable. "I'll get clay on you. If you're wearing something you don't want ruined, take it off and put it in the closet."

I removed my shirt and shoes. I had my pants open when I thought she might be offended. I pulled them back up and cringed as I tried to keep my fly from making a sound she might hear. She stood in front of me, her eyes roaming the room.

"If it's okay with you, take off your pants," she said. "I'll need to check out that famous scar of yours."

My pants went in the closet with my shoes and shirt. Feeling silly in boxers and black socks, I pulled the socks off too.

"You can sit on the chair. Read, or I can turn on the radio. Try to be comfortable."

I sat on a paint-splattered chair, knees quaking and stomach clenched. Hiko laid out chunks of clay and a bucket of plaster. She called this "sketching."

"What sort of pose do you want?" I had an image of Greek statues, Olympian feats or godlike poses.

"I don't work like that. I just read you here and I feel you. I'll do different casts of your body. That's why you'll have to come back several times. If you don't mind."

"I don't mind." I had nothing else to do.

She prepared chunks of clay, lay them in rounded hills on the table, covered them with wet cloth. "Those are for tomorrow." She ran her hands under the faucet and said, "Come here, please."

I came as asked and, when we were close, her eyes fell onto my face. They couldn't see me, but it didn't matter. My heart stopped for a moment. She held out her hand, palm up, and very quietly said, "Put my hand on the scar."

I took her hand and looked down at my leg where the shiny purple lines ran from the middle of my right thigh up and under toward my crotch. I began to lower her hand toward them. The moment she touched me I felt naked.

"Don't be nervous," she said. "I'm not sharp." She laughed.

Her hand stayed for a long time on my scar. I wondered what she read through it. She laughed to herself and then said, with a sense of awe, "I want to do a full body cast of you."

I grew claustrophobic at the idea.

"We'll work up to it," she said. "I'll start with your chest and back." This would, she said, allow me to move my arms and legs. I would be able to breathe normally. Just some plaster bandages draped over me. Like a spa.

She asked me to lay a quilt on the floor with plastic tarps placed over it. The quilt looked made up of old, ugly neckties that individually would make you nauseous but together created a sense of home. I wanted to feel the old, worn silks but they were under the clear plastic. It looked like a museum piece.

Hiko ran a bowl of warm water. Rolls of plaster-wrap bandages sat on the floor near the tarp.

"Shave your chest, and I'll do your back. The electric razor is on the table." I found a man's electric shaver. I wondered whom it belonged to. I did my front, down to my waist. As she worked on my back she said, "You're already so smooth. This almost isn't necessary."

I lay on the tarp and she dropped the strips of plaster into the bowl and then spread them over me. She hummed along to the radio, pop songs and ads, pointless melodies that made me lose my concentration. On my back I tried to remember all that happened, to keep the moment forever. She dipped foot-long lengths into the water and listened to the dripping on the tarp. The plaster was warm against my skin. Her eyes were open, but they glanced upward. Her hands played over my skin as she found the next area to cover. I could see up under the edge of her shirt and follow the curve of her stomach under the cotton.

The plaster built up until I had a heavy covering, an armor plate from shoulder to shoulder, down to just below my ribs. She pushed her hand against my right side.

"Did you ever break your ribs?"

"I don't know. Maybe. I was hit by a bus a couple weeks ago."

"Oh my God. Are you okay?"

"As far as I can tell."

The bus had come out of nowhere. I guess I wasn't paying attention to the traffic. The corner of Broadway and 57th is always crowded. Maybe I'd become distracted; maybe it was the woman in cutoffs and a halter top in front of me. Sometimes in the city I move with the crowd like a bird does with the flock. I trust the crowd, not even really thinking about it. Sometimes the crowd fails me.

I had stepped off the curb and the bus hit my entire left side. If it hadn't been slowing for a stop, I might have been killed.

I'd looked up at the bus. The windshield reflected the neon lights from the surrounding stores. The colors streamed backward up the front of it and, just visible at the center, the driver shouted obscenities at me.

Hiko dipped her hands in clean water at the sink. "Are you okay with the plaster?"

"I think so. It is tightening up. It's a little hard to breathe."

She knelt by me and caressed my face, her nails pulling quietly from my ear to my chin. "It will be okay. Just breathe with me." She lay down beside me. At a right angle to me, with her head next to mine, her temple resting against the top of my head. Her fingers played with my neck and cheek. "It won't take long. Just another thirty minutes or so. When it feels cool."

We lay next to each other. She rubbed my head, and I fell asleep.

Later in the week Hiko shaved both my legs from

the ankle to my upper thigh. I offered to do it, but she insisted. As she worked on my left I watched the razor pull across the hairs and reveal the purple bruises underneath. She traced along my leg with her left hand as her right slid the razor over my skin. "We don't want to have to yank your hair out. If I don't take them off this way, they'll be pulled out by the plaster."

I sat on the edge of her tub. She knelt in it, in ankle-deep, soapy water.

I asked her, "Will this itch when it grows in?"

"I don't think so. You aren't very hairy." She used a light green lady's razor. When I asked if she'd gone out to buy it just for me, she said no, it was hers, the one she used on herself.

"Does this mean my legs will be as smooth and soft as yours?" I blushed, sorry I'd said it. She laughed, her eyes toward the ceiling as she rubbed more soapy water onto my leg below the knee.

"Which leg shall we plaster up first?" she asked. Thunder echoed outside as a rainstorm moved in.

"Right . . . no, left." I wanted to cover the bruises from the bus.

"How about right instead?" She dipped the blade into the water. "It's the one with the scar." She reached for my knee and ran her hand up toward the raised lion lines. She wore black shorts and a blouse covered in small sailing ships. I wore only a T-shirt and jockey shorts, but after her casts of most of my body I felt at ease with even less on.

Hiko drained the tub and began to plaster. She dipped the strips into a bowl of warm water and laid them on my leg. She started around my ankle and under my foot. After an hour I was plaster from hip to heel.

"Try not to move for at least twenty minutes," she said.

"I remember." I'd ruined the first cast of my right arm when a fly landed on my face. I'd knocked myself off the chair and ended up with dried plaster in my eyebrows.

Outside it started to rain. Heavy drops splattered the bathroom window.

"I have windows open. I'll be right back."

She left me to stare at the tub, an ancient, claw-footed behemoth. A dent beneath the faucet mesmerized me, the porcelain chipped and the metal underneath rusted. The mark was shaped like Texas, which was odd because I had slept in a tub in Tennessee with a chip in the same place that was shaped like Louisiana.

At the time, Mal and I had been hitching our way north, to New York, the card Michael now had trembling between my fingers as I played with it in my pocket. I could see in Mal's eyes a distrust of the bloody card, so I kept it hidden and only looked at it when alone, in the bathroom, or when Mal left to look for work or food. Mal avoided all talk of my reasons for going to New York and instead focused on becoming famous. He never bothered to explain what "being famous" meant, only that once I started putting nails into myself it wouldn't take long.

At stops along the way we made money performing in small towns. We found small diners or a mall and Mal would breathe fire or juggle. Then I would pull out the staple gun and make mothers scream while kids wanted to know how I did it. Mal's act would get applause. Mine got us money. Often a simple bet would get us a big meal and a hotel room.

In Memphis we'd made enough to stay in a roadside motel before the police chased us off for not having a street performer's license. We didn't have enough for a room with two beds, so we flipped for who got the tub and I lost. I piled a pillow and some towels on the bottom, with my head at the high end and my feet pressed on either side of the faucet. The bathroom had no window, but some light came through from the room, and as my eyes adjusted to the darkness I saw next to my right big toe the chip in the shape of Louisiana. I had never been there, but I could pick it out on the map.

I'd fallen asleep thinking about Mardi Gras.

I'd woken up to the sound of a door squeaking and opened my eyes. Mal, backlit, stood in the bathroom door. His hand was on the knob, his face turned to the side, as if looking at my feet. I looked down.

A rat chewed on my big toe. Mal watched me be eaten.

I jumped when Hiko's phone rang. It blared until her answering machine picked it up.

I called Hiko's name but heard only the rain on the

window. I lifted myself from the tub and swung my cast over the edge and onto the floor. The hard heel crashed against the tile. I discovered my left leg had fallen asleep and the plaster on my right had fully hardened, making me unsteady on my feet. My left leg tingled as blood circulated again and my right smashed into the wall, the toilet, the door. It swung like a club. Hiko must have used more plaster than she had on my arm because this appeared indestructible and made a solid, earthy thud against everything I hit. I tried to take a step into the hallway and the heel skidded off the floor. I nearly fell. I called to Hiko again and she still didn't answer. I hopped around the corner, looked toward the front door, and saw it standing open. Rain poured outside and the wind blew in. I called to Hiko again. Panic set in. I tried to use the wall as I brought myself stumbling around the corner. I headed for the door at what might pass for running. My left foot caught on the back of my cast and I knocked myself forward, slid on a throw rug, and tripped as I hit the front door. I fell out, headfirst, down the steps. I landed halfway down the front stoop, facedown, just as lightning flashed overhead.

"My God," someone said. I rolled over and saw Hiko standing in the doorway of the building next door to hers. Her neighbor stood with her, just out of the rain. The elderly woman said, "A man with a cast just threw himself down your stairs."

I tried standing and fell the rest of the way. "I'm

okay," I said. I ended up in a puddle at the bottom of the stoop.

"Oh my," said the neighbor. "He's the one I saw on TV." I thought I knew what she was talking about until she said, "You were hit by that bus. Is that how you broke your leg?"

I lay there wondering how she could have known about the bus.

By the time I got back to my hotel several hours later the news clip was running on every local channel. I sat in my room with the television on, the sound off, not really watching. On the screen is a New York City intersection. People gather as cars stream by. A bike messenger nearly clips a guy with a briefcase who turns and shouts. I enter the picture, my back to the camera. I stand behind a group of women in business suits. I look down, step around one woman, and toward the street. A woman in a tank top and tight black shorts runs by and I watch her as I step off the curb. Then a bus enters the picture and hits me. I get knocked to the ground. I could have sworn she was wearing a pair of cutoffs.

NY1 loops its stories, so I watched myself get hit by the bus every ten or fifteen minutes. Each time the clip ended the anchor talked about the weather, or the subway congestion, or city planning projects. I didn't care about that. I left the sound off, waiting for the news to loop back to my clip again, and then I tried not to blink as I watched myself get knocked off my feet, almost gently given the fact that the bus was tons of steel, aluminum, and glass. I wondered over and over: where had the cameras been to film the bus hitting me?

Despite the late hour I called Michael.

"Yeah, I've seen it."

The unexpressed excitement in his voice at the free publicity kept me from asking if he liked it or not. "I don't know how they got film of that."

"There are cameras everywhere. Banks, hotels. It could have been a traffic camera, one that shoots cars running red lights."

"I don't know." *Odd,* was my only thought on it. Was I being followed? Michael, reading my mind, coughed into the phone.

"God knows you weren't being followed. Just dumb luck. You were filmed and now people are talking about the strange man who got hit by the bus and walked away." I remembered him cleaning the spilled coffee, the creation of a still life. "This is good for us. It's part of your story."

On the last day of my modeling for Hiko she took me upstairs to the part of the brownstone where she lived. In the three weeks I'd been going to the sessions there, I hadn't figured out that she owned the whole building.

With the blinds drawn, cool air pooled in the shadows. In the front room she opened the windows and the shades blew in and out with the breeze. The wooden dowels at the bottom struck against the aluminum windowsills, clacking regularly, like people knocking at the sill, begging to come in. Outside, a man hosed the sidewalk and watered the plants in barrel halves on his front stoop. The sound of water spraying against concrete made me feel at ease.

Hiko's soft footsteps padded away from me.

"I want to show you something."

She led me through her living room. It had no furniture except an ugly sofa and a glass coffee table. The walls were all white but covered in stucco with a seashell pattern. In the hallway there were daisies in the plaster. In the kitchen, handprints. I wondered what her bedroom had.

She said, "I wanted to show you the final version of your portrait that will be in my next show." A box covered with a white towel sat on her coffee table. In here she was practically sighted. She moved around easily. She sat centered on the sofa.

She said, "Uncover it."

I lifted the cloth. The frame measured about two feet by two feet, a hand width deep. It held a bloodred mess, a three-dimensional plaster profile. It did resemble me, except that it was red, and broken glass and nails had been mixed in with the plaster. It looked jagged, sharp, and dangerous. It resembled a scab, and an infected one at that.

"What do you think?"

Before I could stop myself I said, "I don't know." I thought she would be offended but Hiko began to laugh.

"Good," she said. "Have you felt it? People have been taught to be afraid of art, but mine needs to be felt. Go on." I put my hand against what was supposed to be my face. The plaster felt cold and smooth in between the glass and nails. Like Braille, I thought. For me it offered only chaotic points, but maybe it meant something to Hiko. I sensed something just under its surface, something I couldn't recognize. It felt angry.

I stood across the table from her, my hand on the face. A question popped out, one that had floated at the back of my head for days, waiting for a moment to come forward. "Why were you ever interested in doing this cast of me?"

"I heard about you from Michael. He was so excited about you. Then I read about you and I contacted Michael and he said this would be good cross promotion. I don't care about that. I just want interesting people to model for me."

"I didn't realize you knew Michael so well."

"We dated a few times. But I got tired of him. No depth. The last time we went out he said I looked like Marilyn Monroe. Why would you tell a blind person they looked like someone they will never be able to get a sense of?" She smiled. "So, that is the piece I'll be displaying."

I ran my hand over it again and felt a catch.

"I think I just cut myself on it."

"You are accident prone, aren't you?"

"I'm sorry."

"Don't be. Now it has your signature on it too."

She stood and walked down the hall and into the kitchen. She returned with a bottle of water, sipped from it, and offered it to me. "Would you like to see the pieces in my personal collection?"

Hiko took me upstairs. In a little room beside the stairs there was no furniture and no lights, just sunlight from an open window. Outside the spraying water had stopped. On the walls were picture frames, the same size as the one downstairs on the long table in front of her ugly sofa. Each frame held a face, or an arm, or a hand over a breast. Each was smooth and calm, lost in its frame, as if wrapped in a womb. Each was a window looking onto someone, or into someone.

"These are mine; they are only for me," she said. She put her hand across me to find the wall and with her other hand she guided me. We took seven steps. I passed a woman's bust, then one showing the back of someone's head, thick dreadlock ropes resting on a shoulder.

She took me to one, slightly crooked on the wall, and said, "This is you."

I stood and looked, as if in a mirror, at my face. My eyes were closed, lips parted. I looked asleep. I looked sad too.

"It's amazing."

"Don't say anything until you've touched it."

I reached up and gently ran my fingers across my cold features. My face held a secret. It looked like a smooth, solid piece of plaster. Underneath the surface, I could feel the tiniest imperfections. But they weren't imperfections. I felt closely, tried to feel between the sensations at the tips of my fingers. She had worked the creases of my skin and the scars above my eyes. She had the cut in my lip and the wrinkles at my mouth. I couldn't see any of these, but I felt them. Just there, under the surface, in the surface. Like a statue put together out of perfectly fitted pieces that could never be seamless. They could pretend, though.

"Two," I said. "Why did you make two?"

"The one downstairs is what they will expect, the one that will be shown and be on the cover. It's for them. This one is for me and for you."

She took my hand and guided me back out of the room, to her bedroom. Without a pause, she undressed. "Are you still bleeding?"

I couldn't stop looking at the curve of her hip and where it wrapped around to her stomach. Without looking at the cut from the first portrait I said, "Yes."

"Did you get blood on the sculpture, on my private one?"

I hadn't. I had used my other hand, just so I wouldn't get blood on it. "Yes," I lied.

"Good," she said. "Lie down."

She walked to the bathroom and when she came back with a bottle she said, "Give me your hand." She sat at the edge of the bed, her toes curling underneath her feet and goose bumps rising on her skin.

I guided her hands to the cut. It had stopped bleeding, and it had closed. Only a half inch long, but I still wanted her to take care of it. She kept her thumb next to the small cut while she wet a cotton ball with hydrogen peroxide.

"It's like you have extra hands," I said. She painted the cut with the cotton. Little white bubbles appeared.

"That's because I need extra hands." She bandaged the cut and said, "Is it too tight?"

I sat quietly, looking at the angle of her neck, the rise and fall of her chest, the white tips at the end of her fingernails, which had paint and clay stuck beneath them. They looked wonderfully dirty. The window blind clicked against the sill behind me.

"No," I said, "it's perfect," and I began to undress.

five

LIVING FOR MORE than a few days in a hotel is like being dead and resting in a morgue. Everything you need is at your disposal, but you need nothing.

Nothing seemed real at the Hotel Thomas. I never watched the television but left it on. I rarely felt like reading but I requested magazines and newspapers that at first piled up, then were replaced with new issues, then were placed in order of arrival, all without ever being read. Once-used bars of soap were switched out for new ones. Clean glasses in tissue paper appeared, lip prints and finger smudges on the old ones gone for good.

I lived in a constant state of consumption. I ruined new things. Such a life is a form of constipation: plenty of effort without any sort of productivity. Food arrived like an offering, beautiful to look at. It left decimated. Porcelain designs were revealed as I ate—a farm scene in blue, trees and fences around the edge of the plate, farmhouse from all sides at the center, animals in a circle, an overhead view of life on a blue farm that only God and I could see from this angle. Chicken carcasses or steak gristle piled at the rim of expensive plates. Tough asparagus or broccoli stems pushed over the edge. Bread crumbs under the napkin. Little wastelands dripped from my fork or fingers.

I sat in my room over the remains of a meal and stared at the window. The sounds of Times Square reached me, even on the tenth floor, and without looking I knew it was a carnival. The theater across the street was showing a revival of a play I'd never heard of and the audience members lined up outside, whatever the weather, clucking to one another about the opportunity to pay to see it.

Word came from Michael occasionally, work leads here, packets of research there. Mal was right, I did get work. Hiko's sculpture of me made the cover of the *Village Voice*, which raised interest. There were some advertising companies thinking of using me, and an early-morning talk show. Michael promised a "grand opening" of some sort.

I was considered for the cover of *Details*. Michael called to get me prepared for the photo shoot. I kept steering the conversation to Mal, awkward attempts really, his name blurted out in the middle of Michael's detailing time, place, and money. I couldn't help it: even though things had ended so strangely, I still felt that I owed him for both getting me out of Caesar's cage and helping me get to New York. Even if Michael had shown interest, I couldn't have gotten word to Mal. He wasn't at the St. Mark's anymore, and Redbach's bar had been shut down, finally succumbing to the roaches and who knows what else the Board of Health form nailed to the door didn't elaborate on. Michael took my interruptions in stride, always with a smile in his voice, but made no promises. Noticing an intake of breath after a sentence, about to reintroduce Mal into the conversation, I stopped when Michael stumbled over some information.

"We found it. That is, you know, we've located the company that used those cards."

"What cards?" It wasn't that I didn't know what card; it was that for a heartbeat I couldn't stand knowing that I knew. A swallow of air traveled the wrong direction in my chest and my head spun.

"The card you found in your suit pocket. You know. That card with the blood on it."

I tried to say something, to ask a question perhaps, any question; I failed.

The smile on the phone line faltered. "I'm afraid they didn't have any missing suits. They don't think it's theirs. They admit it's their card, but have no idea how it got into your pocket. They'll look through their inventory, make sure it's not missing, but they seemed pretty certain. I'm sorry. Really. Very, very sorry. It seemed like a good lead."

Michael and I listened to each other breathe over the phone. I don't know what he thought, but I felt genuine comfort in being on the line with him. His normal bravado, his confidence, his ability to remedy the ugliness of a situation with his own effortless effort had fallen away and in that moment I heard his compassion and understanding of my disappointment. He felt bad for me, and for that I was grateful.

Michael said, "We'll keep looking, of course. It was only the first, not final, attempt."

"I know. Thanks."

"Don't mention it."

Over several days I watched the windows of the buildings across the street and wondered what Michael had done with the card. I worried that he might have given it to the company that denied involvement; I regretted that I'd given it up. Aware of my obsession, I turned my thoughts to my confusion over Hiko and her invitation for me to move in with her, which I'd been ignoring for a week already. I visited her studio and bedroom most days, and during the spans where her work kept her too busy for the distraction that I must be I wondered why she had invited me to live with her. I worried what I might do to her. Her life was clean, simple. Around my room sat pile after pile of promotional gifts, magazines, shirts, towels, all of which would disappear as soon as I left for more than ten minutes. Women in gray smocks, speaking little English but always smiling, would descend. Perhaps they came from invisible cracks in the walls to clean up after me. I'd become accustomed to not having to touch my surroundings. Objects moved without any action on my part. I consumed dry towels at a pace normally reserved for tissues. How would I live if I lived with her? What would I have? I also didn't know if we should be together. I didn't know if I was good for her.

Nothing was mine. There were things around me—a toothbrush, a jacket, clothes, other objects that would someday be "garbage"—that people would say belonged to me, but in reality they belonged only to some future scavenger lurking in an as yet unmade municipal dump.

Day and night lost their meaning. The lobby, designed to be cut off from the streets, glowed under low-hanging glass spheres. Forty-seventh to the north, 46th to the south, at the west side of Times Square. On the street rumbled chaos. Not in the hotel. Inside hunkered little children inside a womb. No noise, little light. The unnerving electric lights hummed with the same low intensity twenty-four hours a day. Men and women in blue suits hovered behind the counter. Requests were filled before I returned to my room—extra towels, clean glasses, ice—and I'd just asked for them five minutes before. Was the brief wait for the elevator really long enough to take care of this? Did they have a clairvoyant staff? There was only one reason why things could be this way: I was the center of the universe.

Every morning the bathroom looked like a tiled paradise: white, chrome, reflective, cold, dry. I left it damp, foggy, littered with wet towels. Like paradise after the dinosaurs came. Wrappers from the glasses, toothbrush, shampoo, and soap in the garbage or on the floor. Used washcloths on the counter. Toothpaste like bird droppings around the sink edge.

The happy consumption continued as I went to Hiko and she felt me for the sculptures or in bed. She felt me for hours and we would talk. Weather, traffic, the strains of waking up. Sometimes she brought up the possibility of my moving in and I again and again deflected the discussion.

Once, as she was cleaning sculpting knives in a green bucket beside her sink, she said, "Why is it that every time I ask you to move in, you make a joke?"

"Do I?" I said. I knew I did. It even annoyed me that I did it. It bothered me more and more.

"Yes." She ran the water over the stained metal. I could see dents and worn spots on the wooden handles. She had held on to these tools for years.

"Are those knives old?" I asked. "Were they the ones you started with?"

"There you go again." She knocked a spatula against the side of the sink. A dull clang rang out. "You never talk about it."

The water kept running and as it trickled down the drain I stood up and walked over to her. I didn't know what I might say. I touched her shoulder and looked down at the sink. Off her hand, along the aluminum blade of the spatula, and down the drain with the swirling water, ran a thin stream of blood.

"Hiko, you're bleeding." She had a small cut on her thumb, just where the blade had been when she hit it against the sink. I took hold of her hand and washed it with the soap she used to clean her tools.

"These tools are sharper than they look," I said. As I cleaned out her thumb my neck got hot and my face turned red. I had nothing but guilt in me, because when she hurt herself I felt relief that I wouldn't have to talk about moving in.

I returned to the hotel that evening and sat by the window. As usual, I fell asleep in the chair. I fell asleep quickly and early. Exhaustion draped me. I woke shortly after noon the next day. I called for breakfast and then went to Hiko.

This continued for weeks. I wouldn't allow myself to think the word *lonely*. Around Hiko I didn't have to worry about thinking it.

One month to the day that my beer commercial hit the air, Michael called to say that Dave's people wanted me to fill in for Regis, who was filling in for someone else. Regis had just gotten another game-show deal and was on a jet to LA. Dave's producer had told Michael in a breathy voice while on his in-office treadmill that Dave was "just dying" to have me on his show.

"This is it," Michael said. He'd been right: my commercial was a hit. It showed me nail-gunning empty cans of beer to my legs while "Stuck on You" played. A ticker-tape warning scrolled across the bottom of the screen: *Trained professional. Do not try at home.*

The greenroom at the Ed Sullivan Theater was freezing. They asked that I wear shorts and a tank top, to show off my scars, but when my teeth started to chatter Michael ended up telling them I needed a suit.

"I just need pants," I said.

"No," Michael said. "You look like an ass in a tank top. You need a suit. Trust me." To my surprise they brought me a nice-looking gray wool suit from wardrobe.

When the production assistant handed it to me, she said, "Of course, we'll need this back."

As I pulled the suit on over the shorts, a monitor on the wall showed images of the stage being prepared for the show. A dark-haired man in a black jean jacket and sneakers sat opposite me reading a worn copy of *Helter Skelter.* His large glasses had thick black frames that made him look fragile. He grinned at me and said, "Hi, I'm Johnny." He'd had a show on MTV that I could have been a part of, stupid stunts and near-death experiments.

"Hi," I said.

"I'm a big fan."

"Thanks," I said. After a moment I said, "Of what?" I thought back to some of the stupid things he'd done on his show. I wondered if he had as many scars as I did.

Johnny showed a smile nearly more gums than teeth. His laugh made him likable. He never told me what I'd done to make him a fan.

Not counting the commercial, shot in an hour in an out-of-the-way soundstage with a cameraman, an advertising exec, and me with a nail gun, this was my first time on television. It reminded me of the circus. Trying to judge which people are in charge by watching how they behave during the taping of a show is like trying to decide what you want to eat based on your favorite number. I had production assistants on either side of me, both talking at the same time. Their voices made me wish I could put nails in their hands. The blond guy with the headset said something about looking directly into the cameras, and the woman who brought me the suit pointed at two chairs set up center stage.

"How are we going to be interviewed all the way over there?" I said.

"Because if you look right at the camera it looks like amateur hour, so try to look at Dave instead," said the headset guy.

"You aren't," said the woman. She held a clipboard between her knees while adjusting the ponytail at the back of her head. Her blond hair had dark roots.

"What do you mean?"

Johnny stood behind me and said, "Didn't they tell you? We're having a little contest."

Mr. Headset waved to two production assistants as if directing traffic. They came to either side of me and each took an elbow. As Mr. Headset walked away he shouted, "Just pretend you're having a private conversation with Dave."

I was led onstage by the assistants, Johnny still behind me. When the taping began Dave introduced me as "that sideshow freak everyone is talking about," and Paul laughed. I wasn't sure how to respond so I just stood and smiled, waited for further instructions, and tried to ignore the hundreds of people watching me. Finally Johnny and I were asked to sit on the two chairs pointed out to me earlier. In the end, only I actually sat. Johnny had trouble staying down. Around fifty 2-inch nails stuck up through the bottom of each chair. We were going to see who could stay seated longer, Johnny or me. I won. Johnny clowned and the audience screamed. Dave offered him a new chair.

"No, Dave, I think I can do it," Johnny said. He took off his jacket so it wouldn't get damaged. "Man," he said to me, "you are for real, aren't you."

I held a magazine, a *Rolling Stone* with Johnny on the cover, chest sprayed with a target and pelted with paint pellets. The magazine prop had been handed to me by a pretty, blond, large-breasted assistant producer with a warning to not "get any freakin' blood" on it.

"Are you sure you'll be able to sit?" she had asked. "When you sit down, open this up and pretend to read it." She had walked away without waiting for an answer. I felt like a mannequin.

Johnny jumped off his chair again. He laughed hard, his glasses nearly falling off his nose. "Man, this is . . ." I could tell he censored himself. "It's very painful, Dave."

"Uh-huh." Dave sat behind his desk, hand on the coffee mug stagehands kept filled for him. Steam floated off his drink. He looked as if he were watching the evening news. "Hey there, buddy," he said to me. "How are you doing?" Other than introducing me, he hadn't said two words to me. I felt like I had to do something to make everyone there realize I wasn't an idiot.

I glanced over the magazine, gave a comic look, and said, "Oh, I'm fine."

Slowly, I sank onto the nails. They weren't close enough together and had pierced my skin. They pushed into my ass like needles into a cushion.

Dave said, "Well, ladies and gentlemen, don't let anyone tell you that we don't provide highbrow entertainment. We'll be back in a moment. Thanks, guys."

"No problem, Dave." Johnny stood rubbing his butt through his jeans. The band kicked in with "Stuck on You," and the lights came up. Stagehands ran over and one grabbed Johnny's chair. The other started toward me but stopped. The assistant producer returned and without looking at me said, "Get up, your segment's over."

When I remained seated, she said, "Why won't this guy get up?"

"I'm stuck," I said. Johnny laughed so hard he nearly fell down.

A couple stagehands pulled me off the seat. They lifted me straight up. "I think he's ruined the suit," said the producer after I stood. The audience applauded politely and there were some laughs and gasps when I turned around and they saw the damage to the suit. Threads hung from the seat of the pants, dangling down the back of my legs. Skin was visible through the tears and blood trickled to my knees.

"Get off the stage," the producer hissed. "We're coming back on."

The lights went down on the stage and the audience giggled at the threads hanging from my legs when the taping started up again. Dave ad-libbed over my exit. "Ladies and gentlemen, some guests just love to stick around. I'm sorry, that was awful. Paul, what the hell is wrong with me?"

Paul pulled his mike toward him and said, "I'm sure I don't know." The audience laughed.

I returned to the greenroom to find Michael arguing with the assistant producer. "But he didn't even want to do the stunt, and if he hadn't been told to wear shorts and a tank top he wouldn't have had to borrow the suit in the first place."

"What's going on?" I asked.

The assistant producer wouldn't look at me, and Michael appeared embarrassed when he said, "They want you to pay for the suit."

I had been used like a toy, and they wanted me to pay them for it. "Tell her to send me a bill." Michael started to protest, and then I looked at him in a way I didn't know I could. I felt pressure build between my teeth, and the muscles at the sides of my jaw burned. "Let's just get out of here."

Michael nodded. I took off the jacket and realized that if I was paying for it I might as well keep it.

Johnny stood in the doorway, smiling to himself. "That suit looks like it was made for you."

I walked out and down the hall, grabbed Mr. Headset's arm, and asked for the nearest exit. I went the direction he pointed. I thought of what Mal might have done if it had been him instead of me, and, convinced he wouldn't have been in the studio to begin with, I reprimanded myself. I'd found the lion's cage all over again, a spectacle at my expense.

Moments of self-recrimination are blinding. I walked, steady, certain, and without thinking. When it became too dark to see I looked up and realized I was lost somewhere behind the main stage. I heard Dave on the other side going through the night's top ten list. Occasionally there was laughter or applause. I tripped over a cord, unsure of where to go, and, as I stumbled, I pulled on a backdrop panel that slid down behind me like a wall.

Unable to go back the way I had come, I worked my way through cables and around a large box. Just as I realized that the large box had windows like a building and that I was about to step on the Brooklyn Bridge the audience roared. I looked up to see the back of Dave's head. Beyond him were lights and beyond that I could only sense the people in the audience.

I'd worked through to the edge of the diorama behind Dave. I stood in a spotlight, complete darkness just past the ring of light. A heavy panel created a blind that hid me from view until I stepped around it. When I realized it was too late for me to creep away, I made the best of it.

"Quite a view you've got here, Dave."

Dave grinned at me and said, "Yeah, except I've got nosy neighbors."

The same assistant producer who wanted me to pay for the suit escorted me and Michael to the exit. She wouldn't look at me but chattered nonstop, as if we were friends. She pretended not to notice the two large security men behind us.

"So, this should air tonight, with a little editing." She shook my hand without looking at me and said to Michael, "We'll send you the bill." At least they didn't ask me to pay for the damage to one of the bridge's stone support columns, nor had they noticed the small guitar-twang tones of miniature cables snapping underfoot.

Security opened the side exit doors and we stepped

out onto 53rd Street. The sun had just gone behind a cloud but the heat rippling off the street hit us both. Michael took a moment to straighten his tie and put on a pair of expensive-looking sunglasses. "I guess we hail a cab?" I said.

Michael looked up and down the street. "Let's walk over to Broadway."

By the time we got back to the hotel the holes in the back of my pants were starting to widen and Michael talked me into getting up to my room as fast as possible and then sending my pants to the hotel tailor.

"These aren't even my pants," I said.

"You just bought pants from Dave, and you aren't going to throw them out. Get upstairs, have them fixed, and I'll talk to you later."

I went upstairs and sat in front of the window looking out at Times Square, the Barrymore Theater across the street, the lines of people dressed up for an evening show.

This is what my life will be, I realized. Michael would take me to meet executives from Budweiser, Coca-Cola, or TD Bank and convince them I could say lines like "Make banking painless!" I would stand in rooms full of business suits in my mended suit with stitched-up legs or nail holes in the ass. They would tell me how much I was needed to sell something for them. We would munch overheated appetizers. Company people would circle into groups and I, a foreigner among them, would not speak their language or know their customs. I would have no place of my own. And when the meetings and dinners were done, I would come back to a hotel room to find nothing as I left it. New soap and cups and bedsheets. Paper napkins folded on the sink counter, and a new newspaper placed neatly on the table. No dirty clothes or used tissues or dog-eared magazines.

Outside a woman stumbled on the curb and fell into the street. A cab honked at her as she caught herself on its hood. I watched, silent, as silent as the other pedestrians staring at the woman pushing herself from the hood of the car, and saw myself as if I had just toppled into traffic, saw myself as both the spectacle and spectator. I realized that Hiko would not clean up after me. She would allow me to sit in my own mess. She would not watch and gawk and stare as I fell from curbs and punctured old wounds. She would not judge. She would take me off this road with this hotel and the circled groups of ad men and give me a place to call home. I called her and heard her smile through the phone when I said, "Let's talk about me moving in."

six

MY FIRST PUBLIC event organized by Michael was Hiko's showing. The "public" piece of me she'd made was displayed along with a dozen other pieces completed in the past year, and Michael made sure not only that would it be talked about but that *I* would be talked about by being there.

The showing was at a Soho space, a former warehouse that had been three different stores/galleries/restaurants before it became this current gallery/performance space. I thought it might become a J. Crew outlet at any moment, with most of the guests staying on as mannequins. The room only barely smelled like wet paint, just under the incense that someone burned through the evening despite Hiko's complaints.

True to her word, Hiko had the red portrait of me on the wall. I thought of it as the scab me. As far as I knew, no one but me had seen the other portrait. The scab hung among other portraits and scenes that relied so much on touch and yet still retained a pleasing look. I stayed in the background as much as possible. I ate crackers and drank martinis.

I eavesdropped, listened in on compliments and complaints about the work, and discovered that I am really bad at eavesdropping. Twice people I was listening in on walked away, and once the conversation turned to how it looked as though I was trying to listen in on the conversation. After that I hung out near my portrait, but no one remarked on it. I marveled at Hiko's talent and how many people came out for her work.

After taking a second martini—I wasn't asking for them; the bartender simply ignored what I ordered and made me one—I walked around the perimeter of the room to find someone to talk to. I checked on Hiko. She sat with Michael and a photographer. Michael made strange, violent gestures with his hands and then looked over at me, smiled, and pointed. I made a noncommittal thumbs-up gesture. I decided I needed some fresh air and hurried to the door as the photographer took aim at me.

Empty plastic bags blew down Water Street. A few people walked by, hands in pockets, blown in the same direction as the wind. I joined them and shuffled to the corner, crossed, and came back on the other side of the empty street. I watched the people inside the gallery. I'd met some of them before, through Hiko or Michael. A reporter from the *Voice* was there and that photographer Michael wanted to sic on me. Even though this was Hiko's evening Michael wasn't above buzz creation. I'd seen the article about the show in the paper earlier in the week, and I would never tell Hiko that it had mentioned me as much as it had her. Michael used our relationship to our "mutual advantage," he said. I didn't stop him and I didn't know why.

As I prepared to return to the gallery, a badly beaten Dodge van pulled up and parked in front of a fire hydrant. It idled loudly for a moment and then the rumble stopped as if the engine had popped out of existence. The side door slid open and a man with long reddish hair lurched out. He turned and helped a thin blond woman in a long, tight paisley skirt pull herself out. Two men climbed out the back. The driver, a man with a shaved head, walked around the front. He said something to the others. The hairy headful glanced over his shoulder at me. From the light coming through the large windows of the gallery I could just see the side of his face, and it took him getting close enough for his features to make sense, with his hair ponytailed on top of his head and a black T-shirt that read IMPEACH PEDRO. He was and he wasn't the man I'd last seen at the hospital.

Mal stroked the long whiskers that hung from his chin. "Miss me?" he said. I felt vaguely threatened.

He turned away for a minute and waved the others into the gallery; all but the blond woman went in. Instead, she walked over, beautiful with her long hair in duplicate braids on either side of her head and her skirt wrapping her to the ankles. There were circles under her eyes and she wore the highest platform shoes I'd ever seen.

She looked me up and down. The tiniest smile came to her lips. "Is this him?"

"Yeah, this is fucking him."

Mal had grown his beard long. Tied into a rope with red hairbands every few inches, it reached the center of his chest. The beard looked like a hanging string of beads streaked with red, brown, and black. His hair was long too. It probably would have reached the middle of his back except it was all gathered in a tremendous clump on top of his head. It stood straight up and fell back, like a little pom-pom. His eyes were dark. He stood as if his back hurt.

I stood at the curb with him, uncomfortable and self-conscious.

I said, "It's been a while." I pointed at his beard. "It's gotten long."

"That's all you can say?" he asked. From his crooked grin a chipped tooth shone in the gallery lights.

"What am I supposed to say?" I sounded angry. I think I didn't know why.

He shrugged. "This and that. You know." He thumbed

toward the gallery door. "You've been busy, getting in with the in crowd." He pointed at my suit. "What did that cost you?"

"I don't know," I said. It had only cost me my dignity. "It was a gift for a show I did recently." I became aware of the stitched holes on the seat of my pants.

"You were on television, right? I heard that." As I nodded, he laughed. Through his smile I could hear the grinding of his teeth. "You did it, man. King of industainment. Go-go-go! I told you."

"Told me what?" I regretted that we were talking. His being there surprised me, but his anger unnerved me. I'd convinced myself that his attitude in the bar on the last night I'd seen him had been an aberration. The result, I thought, of too much alcohol and too little sleep, maybe too much time together on the road. But here he was, still ready to swing at me if only he was holding a hammer.

"I told you that you'd be okay. You've taken off and now you don't need to worry about anything, right? They've got you in some hotel and you're whoring yourself on TV. So, it's all good, right?"

"What are you doing here?"

Mal said, "We're on the guest list, man. Well, Karen here is." He pointed to the girl, as much of an introduction as we would get. "Karen is becoming a pretty well-used reporter here in the downtown scene. Though none of us are VIPs, not like you, Mr. Late-Night Famous."

"I'm not famous."

"Not famous. Your face is on every magazine. You're selling beer on the subways, man. King of New York." He looked awful. He'd lost weight. Long scars littered his arms.

I asked, "What's your problem?"

He looked away and muttered something under his breath to Karen. She shook her head and whispered back. I asked him to repeat himself and Mal looked me straight in the eye and said, "A man who plays with nail guns wants to know about my problems."

Michael came out of the gallery, tilting from too much wine. "Who is this?" He stood unsteadily between us. "A friend?"

"That's one way to put it," I said.

Mal looked down at his feet. "There are probably better ways, though." He laughed. A breeze blew and the reek of the garbage bags on the street hit us. "Shit, that's awful. Let's get inside." He took Karen's arm. "If we stay out here, we might have to rumble."

Michael and I followed him inside. Michael leaned close to me, wrapped me in wine vapors. "Who is that clown?" I didn't answer.

Mal and Karen walked through the gallery and I stood at the front door a moment so I could watch them. I felt like I had just stepped back into the lion's cage. They walked past the guests and onlookers as if they'd been there before, and Mal even seemed to know many of them. He stopped to talk to the bald guy who had been driving the van. I realized then that it was Redbach. He had the same dark eyes and stiff movements as Mal. With his head shaved he looked like a mental patient, and a scar I hadn't known he had ran from his right temple to just above his right ear.

Within five minutes, Mal and Redbach had swept over to the bar and commandeered a bottle of vodka, which they splashed liberally into tall glasses of ice. Karen was nowhere to be seen.

I tried to act casual. I stayed close to the wall and spied on them as they ate and drank. I moved forward as much as I dared, between a group of uncomfortable patrons and my scab self. I tried to look like part of the group, who, speaking only German, made some comments, then left me where I stood.

I wanted to get Hiko and leave.

She sat near the bar, on a small bench, alone. She looked tired and a little sad. When I got to her, I said, "We should go."

Immediately she brightened and said, "There you are." She patted the seat next to her and when I didn't sit she said, "What's wrong?"

"Nothing. It's just that you look tired." I saw Mal look at me and Hiko with interest. He muttered to Redbach; it looked like he was preparing to come over. I didn't want to see him again and I didn't want him to talk to Hiko. I thought Hiko might get hurt by my knowing him.

I didn't know why I felt that way, but it was clear in my mind that something bad would happen.

"Come on, why don't we leave?" I took Hiko's hand and gave as gentle a tug as I could manage.

Her face tightened. She tried to smile. "We haven't been here for very long, and it is my opening. I can't leave yet, and besides, I don't want to. There's someone I want you to meet."

Karen walked up just then, calling out to Hiko. She carried two drinks. "I have a drink for you. Hold out your hand." She kept a martini for herself and handed the cosmopolitan to Hiko. Karen guided it to Hiko's palm, waiting for a small moment until Hiko pulled it away. It had an ease that came from practice. They knew each other.

"I didn't know she was coming tonight," Hiko said. "This is my oldest friend, Karen."

Karen sat in the seat Hiko had saved for me. "We met outside, sweets." She winked at me over her drink. "I'm just so glad that my editor allowed me to switch stories so I could cover your opening." She took Hiko's hand. I stood there, struck dumb, and Mal walked up next to me. Had he planned this? Had he learned about my relationship with Hiko and found a way to connect himself to me through her? How could he have just casually met and gotten involved with Hiko's best friend?

Karen said, "Hiko, you remember my boyfriend." They had met. When, I didn't know, but suddenly it seemed that Mal's plan, if he had one, included Hiko. I called myself paranoid and then remembered that a paranoiac is only someone who hasn't yet been proved right.

Mal gave me a wide grin as Hiko said, "Mal is here?"

Mal said, "I'm right here, Hiko. The only thing more stunning than your artwork is you." Hiko blushed and Mal took her free hand and kissed it just above the knuckles.

Hiko laughed. "I'm so glad you could come too."

I felt like I might pass out. I muttered, "I need a drink."

Mal laughed. "I'll get one with you."

We walked over to the bar where Redbach stood quietly, drinking from the vodka bottle and looking at the track lighting above him. Mal asked for a couple of glasses of ice and poured us each a healthy dose. "Here's to Hiko's opening."

"How long have you known Hiko?"

"I don't know. I met her a couple weeks ago."

"Did you know that I was living with her?"

"Karen said something about that, yeah."

"So you could have contacted me? At any time. But you didn't."

"I didn't think you would want to hear from me." His face dropped into a parody of concern and piety. "What's great is that we have this opportunity to repair our friendship." His sappy grin broadened and Redbach started to laugh, nearly choking on his shot of vodka. To Redbach Mal said, "What, too sarcastic?"

I swore at him and then downed most of the drink he'd poured me. "Just don't screw tonight up for her. She's worked very hard."

"Don't I know it. Hiko and Karen go way back, and Karen's always telling me what a great artist she is. You know what respect I have for great art, great talent." He finished his drink. "Like you, for instance. I see your face on billboards from time to time. That's pretty—how would you put it, Red? Larger than life."

"Sounds about right," Redbach said. The track lighting held some glorious fascination for him.

Mal poured himself another drink and refilled my glass. "Listen, I don't want to ruin anything for anybody. You and I, we can put what happened behind us. You don't need to worry 'bout me hammering you to any of the stuff in here. We can just, you know, start over." From the look in his eye I thought he might be serious. I wanted him to be serious.

"Start over? I don't even know what happened."

Mal picked up his drink and pulled his finger through circles of condensation left by the glass. I realized that the last time we had talked it had been just like this. Us on one side of a bar, Redbach quietly standing by, and a crowd surrounding us that we could have done without. Not looking at me, Mal said, "I was in a bad place, man. I'm better now. And I'm sorry."

I tried to imagine how he could be in a better place when his face looked so much older and so tired.

He handed me a card with his name and number on it. It said HYPER-DRAMA beneath his name.

"What's this?"

"Call me sometime. I'll make you a part of my life again. You can star in the movie that is me."

Redbach checked his watch and made a move toward the door. Mal got up to go with him. Mal whispered to me, "In fact, you can start now. Can you get away?"

Get away, I thought. *From what?* "Away?" I said. Behind me, Hiko laughed with Karen. "Where are you going?"

"The Manhattan Bridge."

I couldn't just leave Hiko. But then I looked over at the crowd that surrounded her. Again, I felt as uncomfortable as I had when we'd first arrived. She drew people to her, she spoke and people laughed, she moved through crowds with humility and was treated like a queen. I only felt more on display. Mal planned to disappear into the darkness, and disappearing held attraction. Even my fear of what Mal might do, and what he'd done to me in the past, didn't keep me from following him. I still preferred the danger that he promised more than the hesitant comfort I felt around Hiko.

Mal walked to the door; Karen stayed behind. I walked quickly after Mal, feeling as though I was cheating on Hiko.

“How long is this going to be?” I asked.

“Thirty minutes. Forty-five at most.” He saw me looking back at Hiko and Karen and said, “They won’t even know we’re gone. Be back in plenty of time.”

I was a little scared to go with him. From the look of his van, I should have been terrified. Redbach got behind the wheel. It came to a rumbling start and a spiral of smoke drifted out from under the hood.

I shook my head. “I should really stay.” I thought if I said it out loud, it would actually happen.

“Still whipped. Just like with Darla.” He turned to get into the van. “You feel anything spheroid grow down there”—he pointed a finger at my crotch—“then you give me a call, okay?”

“You’re sure we won’t be long?”

Mal smiled and said, “If we’re a little late, it’ll be worth it.” He got in the passenger seat and I climbed through the sliding side door. I had to sit in the back on a floor painted electric blue beside boxes of video equipment and cables stacked high enough to promise toppling. Long elastic cords tied in large loops, harnesses, and hooks filled a box nearby.

“What are we doing?”

Redbach smiled and looked at Mal.

Mal said, “Living my life.”

The van died as Redbach started to pull away from the curb, and when he tried to restart it a fresh cloud of smoke poured forth.

"Is this van okay?"

"You're full of questions. 'Are we there yet? Are we there yet?' Just sit down and relax."

I squatted on the box of cables and hung on to the backs of both front seats for some type of stability as Redbach finally got the van started again and we lurched forward.

Over the rattle of the engine I said, "You know, I have an agent who said he's willing to take a look at any acts that my friends might have."

Neither of them responded; I wasn't certain they could hear me over the groan rising from the van. By the time we got to the first light smoke was billowing from underneath the hood. The engine released a loud snap and flames belched at the windshield.

"Maybe this ain't so good," Redbach said. The engine cut out again and as he tried to turn toward the curb the gears seized and the van shook dead, partway through a red light. For a second we all sat there while tongues of fire peeked at us from over the hood. *Like a mirage,* I thought. The cars along the street and the lights on the buildings shimmered behind heat waves. Then smoke found its way inside.

It streamed in through the air vents. The engine let out another loud pop and the smoke turned black and thick. Mal and Redbach opened their doors and I climbed to the back door, knocked the stacks of gear aside, and pushed at the handles. Only one door opened and I half fell out of the van. Mal pulled me the rest of the way.

"Grab something." He pulled at the ropes and rigging near the back. "This stuff is too expensive to burn."

In a daze I pulled rope and backpacks and hard metal suitcases out the back door with Mal and Redbach as the front of the van glowed and burned. All the traffic stopped and someone pulled a fire extinguisher from their car. Thin white foam shot into the flames jetting out from under the hood. It did no good. Fire engulfed the van, the front seats caught, and the smoke became so acrid that my eyes watered. I couldn't see. I backed away and Mal and Redbach tried for another moment to get the last of the boxes. Redbach gave up first. Mal fought the smoke and coughed so hard that spit hung from his lips.

A crowd formed in a circle around us. My mouth tasted like plastic and my eyes still burned. Next to me Redbach doubled over, coughing toward his feet.

Someone pushed by me, a small body but strong. "He's going to die in there." Karen headed for the van. I grabbed her shoulder and she knocked my hand away. "Do something!" she yelled over and over.

Metal and burning plastic fell out of the engine. It smoldered on the street under the van. Black smoke rose above the crowd and spiraled toward First Avenue. Light from street lamps and apartment windows filtered through. Silhouettes floated in windows as the burning van became more interesting than TV. Another fire-cracker pop and the flames began to creep back, under the van and toward the rear. The gas line must have caught.

I could have run to the van and grabbed Mal. I didn't. I stood behind Karen and wondered if he would die. I stood there thinking he might. Everyone stood there thinking it. I took a step forward, unsure what to do. The fire truck arrived.

Two firemen in yellow-and-black hazard gear jumped into the van, and together they pulled Mal out. Another fireman approached with a large canister attached to his back and began to coat the van in thick foam like whipped cream. It piled on so fast that in minutes the entire van became a dessert topping large enough for the entire crowd to enjoy. The circle of people, most of them from the art gallery, applauded politely as the last of the smoke stopped. There were some murmurs about the van not having exploded. I sensed their disappointment.

Karen and I found Mal on the ground near the fire truck, an oxygen mask on his face, which was black with soot; trails of sweat revealed the skin underneath. His hair was partially burned, covered by its own ash, a light orange dust that fell away when he turned his head.

Karen dropped to her knees next to him. "What were you thinking?" His eyes followed her and he smiled as he coughed through the mask. He reached out and took her hand and squeezed it. She repeated the question and then wrapped herself around him, the buzz of a repeated "Oh God, oh God, oh God" on her lips.

Redbach nudged me. "You okay?" I told him I was. "Then you better get over to your old lady." He jerked a thumb in the direction of the gallery. Michael stood with Hiko near the doorway, his arm around her shoulders. When I got over to them she hugged me and then pulled back sharply.

"You smell like an oven." She stepped back carefully, her cane in one hand. "You smell like burnt plastic."

Michael turned his back to Hiko. He whispered to me, "What the fuck happened?"

"I don't know. The van blew up somehow."

"Yeah, I see that, but where the hell were you going?"

"The Manhattan Bridge, I think."

Hiko tapped at me with her cane. "You were going to the Manhattan Bridge?" Her face turned away from me, her ear pointed in my direction, daring me to lie. "During my showing?"

"I was going to come back. I hadn't seen Mal in so long, and we—we were going to the bridge."

Karen came up to us. She held my arm. "Mal wanted me to tell you he's going to be okay. He wants you to call him." Then she took Hiko's hand. "He also wanted me to tell you how sorry he is. They were going to come right back after getting some flowers for you, and then that fucking van blew up. I always knew it was a piece of shit."

Hiko nodded and smiled. “You’re sure he’s okay?”

“Yeah, but he’s going to cough up ashtrays for a while.”

Karen and Hiko hugged and Karen held Hiko’s face in her hands. “Your show wasn’t ruined tonight, honey. It was just too full of energy.” Hiko hugged her back.

Before she went back to the ambulance to be with Mal, Karen looked at me. She said, “Take care of her,” but I felt something else in her eyes. It wasn’t pity, which I’d gotten good at seeing in people. It was anger. It reminded me of Mal from back at the hospital when we’d fought. I had done something wrong in her eyes and it hung there between us as she walked away.

Hiko called to me and I took her hand. As Michael and I led her to the car she said to me, “Were you really getting flowers for me?”

I said, “Why would Karen lie?”

seven

DURING THE NEXT two weeks Hiko's apartment either blazed with light or remained sealed like a dark crypt. When Hiko wasn't there, I left all the lights off. I no longer felt at home. I felt wrong being there after I'd nearly deserted her at her show, so I closed myself off. She was becoming too famous, moving beyond the limited notoriety of art circles. I didn't want to see anything in her house, none of her furniture or sculptures, none of her patterned stucco walls or labeled food cans in the kitchen. It all reminded me of her and the attention she drew to herself, and therefore to me.

When Hiko returned home she would turn on every light, even in the rooms where she wasn't doing anything. She would go into every room, flip all the switches, then leave the room. I never asked why, but when she did this I tried to stay near the front door, as if ready to flee.

The day after the event, Hiko was quiet. She kept to herself in her studio and emerged only to eat. After the sun had set she stood in the center of the dark room as if waiting for spotlights to come on and focus on her. She said, "Odd that you knew Mal. I never would have guessed."

I swallowed hard before answering. I didn't recognize my own voice when I said, "We used to perform in the same circus." I left it at that, feeling it was a lie even though it was factually true.

I thought she could sense the missing pieces, imagined that she had heard from Karen or even from Mal the details I avoided. I expected her to ask for more information. Instead, all she said was, "Isn't it funny how life brings people back to us?"

News of the burning van had been in the papers the next day but soon gave way to other, more interesting accidents. Reviews of Hiko's show hung around a bit longer. Requests came in for interviews and invitations to attend other showings. Hiko was most excited by an invitation to be a guest teacher at the Museum of Modern Art.

"You'll be okay without me at home?" she teased. "All alone?"

"I'll find stuff to do."

She was gone every night for a week.

When alone I made a point of turning off every light

in every room as I moved through the apartment. I ended my wandering in the kitchen. I sat in the dark, a glass of water nearby, and stared at the card Mal had given me. I taped it to the wall above the door, well out of Hiko's reach.

Monday through Thursday I sat listening to music. When the music stopped, I listened to sounds from the street. Michael called early in the week.

"Have some contracts for you. The photo shoot for the cover is coming up in a few weeks. And I've got research material to share with you. We don't think any of it is you, but you never know what might jog your memory, right?"

"Right."

The next day Michael sent the research he and his assistant had gathered in a batch of accordion folders. I don't know how many people were looking into my possible past, whether it was just Michael and his assistant, someone else he'd hired, or a team of unpaid interns. I received pages of photocopied newspaper articles, some from so long ago I would have to be twice as old to match the story. I read about American fakirs, yogis who used pain as a path to enlightenment, who had studied pain meditation techniques in India and returned home, "different" and "wiser," to measure their spirits by hanging their bodies from hooks and piercing their faces and tongues with metal spikes. They spoke of scars as emblems of transcendence.

I read missing-persons reports. Men my age and build, but always with an element, sometimes minor, but more often as obvious as skin color, height, or missing teeth, to demonstrate a difference and remove any hint they might be me. Phone numbers, often the same ones, dotted the bottoms of the reports for tipsters, tricksters, or the bored to call.

Pages of printouts from online search engines stacked two inches high. Questions in multiple hands across the tops of pages or circled around blurred faces in poorly rendered photographs, the red ink bleeding through the paper. Michael or his investigators or both saw any possible connection as a connection. The questions revealed a complete lack of knowing where to start.

Have you ever met the band U2? asked one.

Were you on Star Search Kids? asked another.

I received disks with videos, articles, clippings, bad photos from security cameras. Rumor. Innuendo.

A film crew had once disappeared while shooting a film in north Texas. A freak windstorm had tried to blow Oklahoma into Texas and resulted in dozens of people ill or missing, most just for a few days, but the film crew never returned. I read this story multiple times until I saw a blurred date at the top of the page. I would have been a preschooler.

In the Pacific Northwest a man who claimed to be "going numb" disappeared, an apparent suicide, wandering away from family and friends into the woods. He'd sold all his belongings, all save the suit he repeatedly referred to as his "coffin duster," and when he had finally followed through on his repeated threat of suicide he took the suit with him. The suit had been light gray, with a vest. A picture showed a short, stocky, thick-haired man in the suit. A note in red ink at the side read, *I know this isn't you, but still—???*

I saw myself in all of these. How small a twist it would take to be any of them, I thought, a fiction built out of contradictions. If only I had stopped reading some after the first or second sentence, I could have closed my eyes and accepted the story as my own, gone forward claiming to have discovered something of myself, repeated the tale, embellished, as my own history. A few almost provided smells and sounds as real in my mind as Caesar's cage or the feel of Redbach's bar. Shaking them out proved hard, even knowing they weren't mine, that I had no more claim to them than the readers who took the stories in over morning coffee, muffin crumbs stuck to their chins, gasping at details not because they had happened but because they hadn't happened to them. I couldn't unwatch the footage from a club where a man eviscerated himself onstage. I couldn't remove my sense of fear at the police report of an armed robbery where the suspect fought six cops to a standstill, ignored being Tasered and shot once, then ran through a barbed-wire fence and floated away in a muddy river. I couldn't close my inner eye to the images of car wrecks with no victims present, bloody crime scenes with no bodies.

I kept these pages and disks, these piles of useless evidence in boxes I hid deep beneath my side of the bed. At night I sensed them, heard them settling under me, turning to dust, cracking under the weight of other pages. I lay in bed, not sleeping, thinking of pasts that weren't mine. Figures appeared around my bed: men of various ages, pierced and bleeding, some bewildered and lost, others with a glow in their eyes, flickering with the shivers of pain that ran up their arms from self-skewered limbs and lips. The faces, blurred and obscured, from the photocopies and Web searches, low-quality video and phone video capture, swung back and forth over me, and as they began to speak to one another, calmly, about minor events of their day, restaurant meals, and weather patterns, even as they bled on one another, fell to the floor, and refused any help, they ignored me, to a man. They held their discussions over me and Hiko's sleeping form. I realized I was asleep, dreaming of those I couldn't be, and yet I couldn't wake, not for many hours, as those who bore something so close to me refused to share the secret only they seemed to know.

On Friday Michael and I spoke again. He didn't ask about the research, which was both a relief and a disappointment. Instead, he focused on work. On Monday a photo shoot would take place. "Looks like *Interview* wants you on the cover." He provided the information I needed to find the shoot and I promised to get there early.

"Is something wrong?" he asked.

"No," I said, unsure why I didn't bring up the research myself. "Nothing at all."

That night I leafed through Hiko's Braille books, felt words I couldn't understand. I laid one after another around the living room, on the table and on the floor. I ran my hand over pages and pages of tiny bumps. Maybe I could take the information into my subconscious. I groped my way into her world, but I didn't comprehend the language.

Against the wall opposite the sofa sat a new sixty-inch flat-screen television set. Hiko had suggested that I get one so I would have something of my own. Not knowing what else to get or do, I agreed and bought one. Michael helped me pick it out.

As I knelt on the floor, my hands resting on the pages of Hiko's books, I saw my reflection in the flat, dark screen. I could see no details, only vague shapes, but there I was, fuzzy and dim and distorted. A dark splotch at the center against the white backdrop of the walls behind me. I went to the kitchen and pulled a knife from the cutting board. From the utility drawer I pulled a roll of masking tape.

The Braille books looked like normal books on the outside. The titles were written normally on the covers, and on the bindings as well. Like a person wearing a mask of a smiling face, the true nature of the books lurked deeper. On the inside differences emerged. I looked over the titles until I found one that I couldn't imagine Hiko reading: *Mythologies* by Roland Barthes. It must have been a gift. Flipping to the end, I pressed the knife hard into the crease of the binding and slid it through the pages. I cut away twenty pages, laying each one in front of me until I saw that I had enough.

When I finished, Braille pages covered the television screen. Small loops of masking tape held each page in place. I turned on the television and found a channel with a signal and played with the antenna until the sound cleared. The images illuminated the pages from behind with a wavy, multicolored light. The colors hinted at what the images were but I couldn't be certain what I saw. A woman or a man or a cat or a car, something moved around the screen. Hundreds of bumps across the pages lit up, small explosions of meaning being highlighted. After five minutes of listening to commercials and entertainment news, I turned the set off so that the pages and the room were dark again. I knelt on the floor and placed my hands back on the books.

The phone rang. As I walked to it I said aloud to myself, "Let the machine get it." Stepping carefully around the books, I repeated this. I said it one last time as I picked up the phone and said hello.

"Hey. It's Mal."

For a moment I couldn't think. "I think I lost your card." A lie; the card was still taped above the kitchen door.

"That's okay. You've gotta do me a favor."

I didn't like the sound of that. "What sort of favor?"

"Meet me at the Manhattan Bridge. On the Brooklyn side."

"It's late."

"I know. That's why you'll do it. You've got nothing else to do."

He hung up.

I quickly gathered Hiko's books and put them back on the shelf. I pocketed an extra page cut from *Mythologies*.

In the backseat of the cab I obsessed over why I had agreed to meet him. As the driver headed down Flatbush Avenue, still busy with people, I wondered what makes some people go out and do things while others build shelters and reasons to not go anywhere. I pulled the book page from my pocket and felt the Braille bumps and imagined myself watching television while Hiko wandered around the room, lightly feeling her way past the set with its screen hidden by dots on the pages. I obscured something only I could see with something only she could understand, but she wouldn't notice unless I directed her hands there, unless I brought her to the television—a mostly useless object for her—and laid her fingertips on the screen. Before I could think of what Hiko might say if she discovered the pages, the cab arrived at the bridge. I placed the page into my wallet after paying the cabbie his fare.

At the foot of the Manhattan Bridge, under the

Brooklyn-Queens Expressway sign, Mal stood with seven people. When he saw me, he raised both arms and shouted, "Back from the great beyond."

I wondered how they had all gotten there so fast. "Where's the van?"

Mal let out a deep laugh. "What van?"

His group laughed too. Three women and four men, two of whom had the same hair and beard as Mal. He cloned himself, apparently. They dressed and stood exactly as he did. Even their hair color looked the same. I thought his strangely trimmed, cut short in odd places and randomly unkempt. Then I remembered the fire. He'd lost several inches from different parts of his head.

Mal grabbed my shoulder and led me to the pedestrian walkway over the bridge. "Man, you saw for yourself. That van died a sad death. We're stuck with cabs for the time being."

I glanced over my shoulder at the group following. They carefully watched Mal as he talked to me. They were like Caesar in his cage, scared of me and likely to vomit. I received quick glances but no direct eye contact, nothing in the way of conversation. They avoided me, as if they'd been told I was dangerous.

Redbach reminded me of Yuri the lion trainer. He pushed a cart full of rattling gear covered by a blanket. I could almost believe it hid rancid meat.

The bridge was silent. Leaning over the handrail, I looked down the Manhattan-bound car lane. It was empty. "Where's the traffic?" A woman walking beside Mal laughed.

Mal gave a sidelong glare and said, "They've been closing this down at night for years. Rebuilding." He didn't try to hide the annoyance in his voice. "You've lived here how long?"

"I didn't know."

"Lists of stuff you don't know."

We walked in silence for several minutes. A Q train rattled past. Inside it row after row of empty seats glowed under fluorescent lights. As the last car finally passed us and the noise disappeared with it down the Manhattan side of the bridge, Mal pointed and said, "Dead center, right there." I might have imagined it, but it seemed the wind died as we reached the middle.

At the peak of the bridge, the Manhattan skyline reflected in the water below us like liquid fire, Mal clapped his hands and turned to face the group, a cold and shivering semicircle around him.

"Ladies and gentlemen," he said. In the dark his eyes and teeth shone brightly. "We have gathered here to reclaim our lives, to make our hearts beat, to fill our lungs with air that hasn't been produced or purchased or packaged. Most of you know what this will entail." He looked at me and a couple of the young women with the heavy eyeliner and chattering teeth. "A few of you don't."

Those who knew laughed at those who didn't.

Redbach pulled back the blanket to reveal coils of rope. A lanky guy named Jerry joined him and the two of them unloaded rope and straps and hooks I thought might be mountain-climbing gear. It looked like the same equipment from the van, and I even thought I smelled a hint of burnt plastic.

Mal continued his sermon. "People are claiming unexplored spaces all the time. Think of the millions of people who've walked through Grand Central. Compare that with the few hundred who've walked on the roof of Grand Central. Compare that with the guys who walk high steel. They get to be first. They own that space."

Mal removed his jacket. He stood in a T-shirt and jeans, and there were scars, burns up and down his arms.

"Some of you pay for the right to be here. Some of you don't. Some say that's not fair." He stretched his arms over his head until a shoulder popped. "I say, I gotta eat too." The girls laughed again, poked each other over how cute Mal was, with his broken tooth and burned hair. "If you don't like it, mug one of the guys who didn't pay. I'll let you work that out among yourselves." He winked at the blonde who'd walked on his arm all the way up. He had picked his trophy. I wondered if Karen knew about this.

Jerry knelt before Mal and helped him with the straps. They fit tight around his ankles and were covered with rings and heavy ropes bound through metal clasps.

Jerry focused only on the gear. He'd heard the speech before—or not. He simply didn't need to. He obviously believed in Mal.

They tightened and retightened each buckle, pulled and yanked each strap again and again until they felt no slipping or give. They followed the loops of rope that led through and back again to a main coil at Redbach's feet. Redbach, meanwhile, played the other end around the walkway's metal handrail, tying a thick and complicated knot resembling a fist.

Redbach pulled wire cutters from his back pocket. With three quick snips he removed wire loops holding the chain-link fence to the handrail posts. The fence kept people from jumping off the bridge. He peeled a section three feet wide back like skin from an apple. As he did, he talked loudly, as if to himself.

"Remember that when you jump, arch like a diver, otherwise you tumble, and if you tumble there's a chance of pulling something. And breathe. But not too deep—"

"After all, it is the East River." Jerry finished what must have been an old joke.

Mal nodded without looking at them, then stared out over the river. He nodded again, as if hearing a question no one else could hear. I gripped the handrail hard, whitening my knuckles. Again I felt like I was back at the lion's cage, but this time I was on the outside and Mal was on the inside. I suddenly realized that maybe that was why Mal had come to resent me—he'd grown tired of the worry. Or maybe it was just exhaustion at all the eyes that followed me.

The women had clustered together. Only the tiniest sounds escaped us. A boot scraped on the walkway floor. The blonde sniffed.

Mal rubbed his hands together and dried his palms on his pants leg. Jerry and Redbach helped him climb over the handrail. His legs only spread a few inches due to the cords running between his boots. Redbach and Jerry lifted him carefully, set him in a sitting position on the handrail, and helped him swing his legs over so he faced the water. He sat between the sloping edges of the chain-link fencing. To his right Redbach slowly lowered the coils of what could only be a bungee cord over the handrail until the length of it dangled beneath Mal's feet.

As he sat on the rail, a picture of intense calm, his eyes on the city lights, I felt I had to say something. Only a faint crackling sound escaped my dry mouth. I coughed and tried again.

"What if something happens?"

Mal shook his head. "Well, something is going to happen."

Redbach laughed.

I ignored him. "Is this safe?"

"Nothing is safe." His hands were on the handrail, his knuckles as white as mine. "You should know that."

"As long as we get you out of the river."

He winked. "You will. But keep an eye out for cops. This is very illegal."

His grin lit the crowd. This would kill him. I was certain. Behind his cavalier attitude had to be some realization of his stupidity, this breaking away from reality by leaping into a free fall over the river. I felt sick.

With a tap on Redbach's shoulder he let everyone know it was time. Redbach and Jerry each took a hand and lifted once again, helping Mal to his feet atop the rail. With one hand Mal steadied himself against the fence post. He lifted his other arm straight out in front of him.

The people on the bridge with us fanned out along the rail. The bridge was a rule, a commandment of force and gravity, that everyone had to obey in their transfer from one land to another. Silent, we haunted its steel girders, watched as one of us tried to break free of it. I felt the jagged lift in my legs that I'd had when I faced Caesar, as if being lifted from the inside. I vibrated with it, tensing against it and for it. Behind us the rumble of the next train built. Mal stood completely still for a minute. It took forever for the train to reach us. It crashed toward us, like a laboring spectator afraid to miss the main act. Its noise became deafening, nearly enough to make me look at it, and then Mal said something and smiled to himself. He leaped.

He disappeared into the darkness. I could no longer see him, could only watch the line move and begin to tighten, and I thought that this was how he came in and out of my life: in bursts, at the most unexpected moments. I forced myself to exhale and felt myself lowering down off my toes.

The group remained silent. I'd expected cheers, but none came. Barely a sound could be heard. What little wind there had been died. I looked up at the great metal girder that rose above us and thought of the people who'd climbed it to build the bridge, of the few people to stand atop it. I thought that maybe if the bridge hadn't been needed they would have built it anyway, just to build it. Just because they could. Just for Mal. The ropes around the handrail were tight and creaking. Above the handrail hunkered the city, and beyond the city clung the starless night sky.

From below us came the distant echo of Mal's laugh. Redbach grabbed hold of the rope and Jerry and he each planted a foot against the handrail and began to pull Mal back up. As rope became available each of us took a place behind them, reaching forward to the next hold. The pullback pinned me between Jerry and the woman behind me, who in turn pinned another. Redbach chanted "pull" with each heavy tug, and then everyone would reach forward with one hand, careful not to let the rope slip forward again, to grab the next piece before bringing the second hand forward to meet the first. Bent forward like that, each of us resting against the back of the person in front, we waited for the next cry of "pull" to raise Mal another few feet. We all breathed together.

I don't know how long it took to bring him back to the bridge. All of our hands mixed and grabbed one another, and I lost track of my own, recognized them only by the webs of scars that ran along the edges of the fingers and up to my wrists. No thought, only pulling, the lifting of our friend, and I fell into the rhythm of the group effort gratefully.

At last Mal's hand rose to grasp the handrail. Jerry grabbed him and pulled him over, and both collapsed onto the walkway. Mal laughed. "Took you long enough." He was soaked, having dipped into the river; water dripped from him as he leaned against the rail.

I reached down to help him stand but he remained seated and began to undo the buckles at his ankles. I asked if the line had been too long.

"No, just right. As I got close to the snap-back point I slowed enough to hit the water safely. I went completely under, then was pulled back out." He grinned up at Redbach, who grabbed his shoulder and shook it.

Redbach said, "Told you we had the right length."

Mal squinted at him. "I'll tell you something, though. That water burns your eyes. Pollution's a bitch."

Mal worked himself out of the bungee harness and conversations picked up. Everyone had thoughts about what his jump meant. Opinions differed: some found it important as a cultural statement, others an entertaining diversion. The group mind fell away. We'd all begun to think again. I thought it was Mal just being Mal, true to his nature, putting himself where other people wouldn't. He looked me in the eyes and laughed and said something blasted away the moment it left his mouth by the thundering roar of a police chopper. Helicopter spotlights beamed down at us and everyone scrambled like roaches.

Mal, Jerry, Redbach, and I ran to the Manhattan end of the bridge. Everyone else headed back toward Brooklyn. I looked over my shoulder and saw the light dance over the latticework like fingers on a body. The glare receded, following the others. The helicopter turned away, its thunderous beating of the air softened. We ran toward Manhattan, our breath heavy and our footsteps irregular and pattering as rain.

Jerry gasped and tried to speak. "As long as they don't have units waiting down here, we should be okay."

To make sure we weren't being followed I looked over my shoulder again. I saw the chopper far away over the Brooklyn edge of the bridge and turned back, just in time to see the girder I was going to run into.

After the impact, I turned in a slow circle without light or sound. When I opened my eyes, Mal stood above me. He laughed.

"What's so funny?"

"You just asked me if the lion is okay."

"I did?"

"Yep, but that's the wrong ending, my friend." He helped me stand, and Jerry stuck a hand under my arm and we took off again. Everyone looked concerned. Everyone except Mal.

"Cops might be at the end of the bridge," Mal said. "Can you run?"

"I think so," I said. And we did. Blood kept spilling into my eye from a cut. My brief loss of consciousness had been restful. No pain, of course, just a sudden sleep. I had never done that before.

We arrived in Manhattan panicked and flying on foot, jumped over a wall onto a side street next to a weedy little park where junkies were shooting up, and then rushed into a subway station. We didn't see any police, but we weren't going to wait for them. I fell down the stairs and the others carried me part of the way, past the row of automated MetroCard vending machines. I could barely hold my head up. I must have hit it pretty hard.

"I think I'm hurt," I said.

"You are losing blood." Mal pressed a hand to my forehead.

"Christ," Jerry said. "How can you stand? I think you've got a concussion."

Mal smiled.

A train pulled into the station and as I staggered on board the conductor shut the doors on my foot, tripping me. The empty car smelled recently used.

Mal and Jerry helped me onto a bench and laid me down. Mal was still wet, and began to shake in the train's cooled air. Still, he took off his sweatshirt and put it under my head. "You don't know who we've got here, do you, Jerry?"

Jerry shook his head as he knelt beside me, examining

my forehead. He looked into my eyes and asked me to follow his finger. It passed back and forth in front of my face.

"We got a real live famous person here. You remember the guy who can't feel pain, the one everyone's gaga about?"

"No shit," Jerry said. "It's a pleasure." Using a penknife from his pocket, Jerry cut away the edge of his T-shirt and folded up the fabric. He pressed it against my forehead. The train seemed dim and I couldn't be sure I wasn't passing out. "We gotta get these cleaned," he said. "I think you split your kitty."

"My kitty?"

"Yeah. This nice cat scar you got up here."

Redbach left from the subway to go to a drugstore for some bandages and alcohol. Mal and Jerry pulled me along Hudson Street and into Jerry's apartment building. His apartment had a long, narrow hallway at the end of which sat the bed in the main room. A heavy-hipped woman in a T-shirt and running shorts didn't look up from her magazine until she realized I was bleeding my way into her home, then she became all questions and concern, running around the room to get gauze and peroxide.

Jerry made me sit down. When I did, I saw the mirror beside the bed and my wounded reflection. My forehead was split open above my left eye, right across the Garfield scar. A two-inch gash and several smaller cuts covered what had been an eyebrow. Rust-colored dust painted half my face. There were three evenly spaced bruises forming on either side of the cut—probably from bolts in the girder.

The woman stood over me, looking at the gash. "Hi, I'm Debbie. Jerry's wife." She took away the shirt-bandage and began to clean the cut with water poured from a bottle. Bloody water washed off my forehead and onto the bed. I tried to warn them about stains but they wouldn't listen.

Jerry rummaged through the closet and brought out what he called his "stash," a large duffel bag from which he pulled a hypodermic needle.

I couldn't imagine what narcotics they thought I needed. "I don't use anything. Besides, the pain isn't a problem."

"No, but the rust is. This is a tetanus shot."

"You keep that in your stash?'"

"You never know when you might happen upon a rusty nail, my friend." He jabbed me in the arm while Debbie pulled and twisted my other appendages, looking for more injuries.

"Let me know if this hurts," she said as she squeezed my right knee. Mal winked and said, "Ouch."

It turned out that both Jerry and Debbie were EMTs, and Jerry even had a degree in nursing. As Jerry sewed up my cut, Mal and I talked. Mal was finally warm in a fresh pair of jeans and a clean T-shirt from a bag he'd left with Jerry earlier. We sipped at some coffee and I realized that we hadn't talked this casually since leaving the circus.

"You need to come around more often," he said. "I'd forgotten how much fun you can be."

He reached into his bag and pulled out a blue T-shirt. Superman's S stood on the chest.

"What's this?"

"Now you can be my sidekick, my Superboy."

Jerry drank a beer while pulling sutures through my forehead. "Superboy wasn't a sidekick. He was Superman when he was young."

Mal's face paled and his lips disappeared as he tensed. "Who was his sidekick?"

Jerry thought about it. "Didn't have one. Not like Batman. Not regular. Jimmy Olsen? But he doesn't really count."

"Why?"

"No costume, no powers, no consuming need to be a hero."

Mal stared at the line of black threads sewn into me.

Debbie cleaned blood out of the washcloth in the bathroom sink. Mal's clothes were piled in the tub behind her. They smelled of sewage and she made a face at us from the doorway. "How can you stand to dip into that river water?"

Mal spoke over the edge of his cup. "It's a necessary evil."

Jerry said, "Practice makes perfect." He snipped the thread he'd just knotted above my eye. "You're done."

I decided I didn't want to know what Jerry meant by practice. There were so many questions I could have asked, but I was more interested in being accepted by the group. They were odd, maybe a little dangerous, but they had taken me in and made me feel at home. It was like the circus all over again, I thought. It didn't occur to me until later that my time calling Tilly's circus "home" had ended in a lion's cage. Our little group spoke until early in the morning, not about any one thing or even things worth remembrance. Remembering the specific words was unimportant. Something unnamable surrounded us, something I couldn't find elsewhere. That we spoke at all seemed key, that we looked at each other and smiled and sometimes spoke over and around ourselves, that we ran out of drinks and food and that by the end half of us were asleep on the floor and that when the sun came up I dozed in a cab rolling over the Manhattan Bridge back to Brooklyn and I could see the skyline as only a cluster of buildings, not stars locked to the ground, that the liquid fire on the water had just been office light reflections, and the rattle of the trains sounded as long and loud when they passed as they had the night before, whether my friend leaped or not.

eight

THE DAY AFTER our run on the bridge I woke in Hiko's brownstone with two swollen, black eyes and a purple lip. The jagged stitches in my forehead were the most casual thing about me. I looked as if I had been hit by a car.

I lay on the living room sofa. I woke just before noon. I could hear Hiko making herself lunch in the kitchen. Without saying anything I went upstairs, showered, and dressed. I thought that making myself presentable and smelling clean would soften my disappearing act the night before.

When I crept down the stairs and found Hiko drinking ice water in the living room, she tilted her head toward me and said, "Did you have fun last night?" No anger in her voice, just the question, and I thought there had to be more than that. Did she know about my black eyes? She couldn't see them. I wondered if I had screamed something in my sleep, some sort of confession.

"I guess so."

"You know, if you're going to go out, just leave a message on the answering machine. I didn't know where you were until Karen called."

Karen had called. "When did she call?"

"Around midnight. I guess it was when she left you and Mal at the bar."

I stepped down the hallway and into the bathroom off the kitchen. In the mirror were my black eyes and the ragged stitches in my forehead. I hadn't imagined it. I had been clobbered by the bridge. For some reason Karen was creating alibis for me. First at the gallery, now this.

Hiko spoke to me from the living room. "Michael called. To remind you of a photo shoot?"

I'd forgotten completely. I called a car service and rushed to get something to eat. On my way out I went to Hiko in the kitchen. I gave her a kiss, certain she could smell the guilt mixed with perspiration on my skin, certain she could sense the bruises on my face.

The photo studio filled the first floor of what had been a warehouse near Chambers Street. Along the walls were giant sculptures and paintings made from found materials. The largest looked like a water buffalo stuck in a gold-leaf frame. It was titled "Self-Portrait."

I was late. I enjoyed a perverse pleasure in making Michael sit and wonder, calling me on his cell phone. He was on it when I walked in, his eyes narrow and lips tight. When I took off my sunglasses his face went blank. He took in my dark-rimmed eyes. "What the fuck happened to you?" he said. "Is there somebody we should sue?"

A woman in six-inch heels teetered toward us. Even in her stilettos she stood five inches shorter than me. She said, "Lord, you look hideous. Is it makeup?" She had on a black suit and the shoes had a leopard print. She set a pile of papers that promised to spill everywhere on a nearby chair.

She flashed her teeth at me. "I'm from the magazine." We shook hands and she leaned in to take a closer look at my face. "What happened to you?"

"I ran into a scaffold," I said.

"Amazing." She smiled at Michael. "We'll have to use that in the article."

Michael immediately shifted from concern to professional pride. "Didn't I tell you? He's fantastic."

She finally let go of my hand. "Grade A, extra large."

Michael pointed out the others wandering around the room. The photographer wasn't much taller than the magazine rep. One assistant adjusted diffusers—large white screens to break up the light—from the top of a ladder. A second assistant teased the backdrop drape over a metal rod that ran the length of the room. They constructed one of those nonexistent neverwheres that magazines all seem to take place in.

Through an open door at the far end of the room I could see several women walking around. Michael grabbed my arm. "Oh, by the way. I think I'm in love with the model they brought for you. She's the set of legs right through there."

We stood at the front of the room watching parts of women flash by the doorway, and Michael told me all he knew about the model, Emilia, whose profile apparently had been on the rise for six months. She had a long neck and thick brown hair and light green eyes. "She's about all I want in life," he said. I didn't know how to interpret that.

The magazine rep appeared at my elbow. "Watch out," she said, a twinkle in her eye. "I hear she's nuts. Likes to get into kinky relationships and ruin the man when she breaks it off."

The conversation in the other room stopped and she stepped through the doorway to meet me. I thought that, since I had seen her on magazine covers before, I would be ready to see her in person. I wasn't. First, her height surprised me. In bare feet she was a couple of inches taller than me. Second, she was stunning—in nothing more than sweatpants and a white T-shirt. I suddenly thought, *She may be all I want in life too.*

She spotted me when she walked in. She said something to the photographer and then Michael took my arm again and led me forward.

"We are going to go talk to her," he said. A command for me or himself? I didn't know.

Soon everyone clustered at the center of the room and we all shook hands, as if I hadn't just done so minutes earlier.

From the back doorway came two more people, a tall blond man with a mustache and a woman who looked like another model.

Michael said, "These are the costumers."

"Costumers?"

The blond man sauntered up to me, held my elbow between two fingers, and guided me to a changing area that was really just a curtain over a doorway. "You'll find it all in there, babydoll," he said. I found "it," a black suit with an Italian name. The tie was Italian too, but no relation.

I stepped out and everyone eyed me and murmured approval. In the mirror by the curtain I looked at myself. It fit me perfectly, made me realize the poor fit of both the suit I'd arrived in and the one purchased from Dave's studio, nail holes and all. Above the handsome suit hung two black eyes and threads poking out of my forehead, almost holding shut the cut greasy with antibiotic ointment.

The photographer called me over and snapped a roll of just me. He didn't ask me to do anything. Instead, he walked around me and held three different conversations with the magazine rep, his assistant, and the blond costumer. Emilia changed behind the curtain, helped by the other costumer into something that made them both swear and laugh. I forgot to smile at the photographer and so most of the photos turned out with me looking distracted. The silhouettes on the curtain had my attention.

At the end of the first roll, Emilia stepped out in a leather dominatrix outfit. The blonde appeared from the hallway with a cardboard disk painted on one side like a bull's-eye. She hung it by a hook on my belt, making me the target, my ass in particular. Emilia held a bat driven through with nails at vicious angles. The photographer took a roll of shots of Emilia reeling back, as if just about to tattoo my ass out of the park.

"Look mean," he told her. "Get it from deep within you. You really want to hit him." He snapped away. "Angry, but with a smile on your face."

Emilia pretty much ignored me. Despite what the rep had said about her and the dominatrix outfit, she seemed pretty normal to me. Not mean at all. She glowed: her parts covered in leather gleamed like a polished floor, parts revealed shone healthy and pink and squeezed out at me, pinned me in place, tacked between aroused and bored.

No one told me to do anything, so I did nothing. I yawned and they took photos of that. I put my hands in my pockets and found two pieces of paper, one a little bigger than the other. While cameras clicked, I took them out and read them. The small one said, *Inspected by Number* 3. The other, handwritten, said, *Just be patient. This won't hurt much. —E.* I laughed and looked at Emilia, who smiled and winked, then poked at me with the bat. It wasn't an angry smile, so the photo was no good for the magazine. It was a nice, genuine, "I'm friendly and I like you" smile.

As the photographer adjusted the lighting, Emilia said, "I enjoyed your film."

"Thanks." I tried imagining which film it might be.

The photographer clapped his hands. "No time for talking. Emilia, change costumes."

She stepped into the changing area and the costume woman practically attacked her. Another batch of giggles burst from behind the curtain. Michael and the photographer smoked and made rude comments. "This is going really well," Michael called to me. "But if you are thinking of having sex with her, you should remember who you're dealing with."

I wished that I was alone. I looked at Michael and thought about what he might tell Hiko. I hadn't thought of her until then and I realized that was probably wrong. In my hand I rolled and unrolled Emilia's note.

I had to confess. I walked over to Michael. "She gave me a note."

"This isn't high school." It sounded like a reprimand. "Don't be silly."

Emilia came out from behind the screen. She wore a fur bikini so small I could tell she shaved or waxed most of her body. She wore a wig shaped like a lion's mane with built-in cat ears. She wore cat's-paw gloves and between her legs I could see a tail swinging seductively.

Everyone laughed except me. I wasn't bored anymore.

"All right," the photographer said as he plucked the disk from my back and attached it to my belt buckle. The target hung over my groin. "Let's shoot some more."

Emilia came toward me, the small triangles barely covering her breasts, a hint of the right nipple peeking out. The fur looked as if it stood on end, like an animal's fur rising as it hunted. Her skin had gooseflesh, the bumps showing from her wrists to her shoulders, and all along her sides, her hips and stomach, down to the very low, arresting triangle of fur at her groin. The fur there was longer than the top piece; she looked almost more like a cavewoman.

"You're cold." I felt stupid for saying it.

"A little." She smiled.

She dropped to her knees, raised her paws in the air, and rested them against my stomach, her mouth in a smile, all teeth. She growled and squinted her eyes playfully.

"Perfect," someone said. For a moment I had no idea who the hell it could have been and looked around the room wondering who these strangers were. Blinded by a flash, I remembered the photographer. I looked back at Emilia and tried swallowing. The flashbulbs popped and the camera clicked away as she clawed at my pants and, despite the clumsy-looking paws, undid my belt. The target fell to the floor at my feet.

Michael said something and the photographer kept taking shots. "Hang that on your chest," Michael said. "On your breast pocket." Emilia picked up the target, adjusted the hook on the back, and snagged it to the jacket's pocket. It hung over my heart. She tapped her claws against it, a light ticking sound, and smiled as she glanced over her shoulder at the camera. She arched her back.

The camera clicked.

Emilia said, "Let's see the scar that big kitty left on you. It's on your thigh, right?"

I muttered a few vowel sounds and futilely tried to push her hands away. Someone said, "I don't think this can be on the cover." Nervous laughter from the spectators, but the camera clicked. She went as far as getting my fly down when I grabbed her paws.

"Let's stop there."

"All right." She pulled the zipper partway up. Running her hand down my thigh, she asked, "It's under here—right?"

I said it was.

"I'll have to see it later." Then she turned her head and bit my pants leg, pulled at it with her teeth. The photographer finally stopped.

"Beautiful." He turned to the magazine editor, who nodded and said that would do it.

Emilia pulled herself away and smiled up at me. "That's certainly enough for me. I'm cold and tired."

Everyone began to pack up. Main lights were turned on. The spots shut off. Michael put on his jacket and finished a conversation with the magazine rep. He gestured at me, then pointed at my pants, at my fly half down and the belt undone, a wet spot on my leg where she had kissed it.

I stood at the center of the room. Emilia changed behind the curtain. She removed her bikini top and the gloves and dropped them into a black bag. She pulled her white T-shirt out of the bag, but waved me over instead of putting it on. She stood half nude. I tried not to stare.

"I want to see you again," she said.

"I live with someone."

She laughed and shrugged, then pulled the top over her head. Her breasts moved gently beneath the white cotton. She still had the furry crotch. I thought maybe it wasn't a bikini at all. Maybe it was just her.

As she pulled her hair back she said, "Bring your live-in lady friend along." Her navel poked out from underneath her shirt and I realized that I wanted to put my tongue in it.

"She's blind." I don't know why this seemed important at the time.

"So don't let her drive." She laughed again. It started and stopped without warning, like a child's. "Give me your number. I've got to go to LA for a week, but when I get back I'll give you a call."

"I don't know."

"Yes, you do. Give me your number."

From her bag she pulled a pen. I found a blank piece of paper in my wallet, wrote Hiko's number on it, and handed it to her. As she read it her fingers brushed over the numbers. "What's this?"

Across the paper were tiny raised dots. I said, "It's Braille." I'd forgotten that I still had the last page cut from Hiko's book in my wallet, never certain what to do with it.

"Cool," she said as she ran her fingers back and forth across the bumps.

nine

TWO DAYS AFTER the shoot, with Mal's help, I tried convincing myself that Emilia would never call. Mal and I met in the Hotel Thomas bar. He unashamedly sat at the chrome-and-glass bar in a T-shirt that said ASSHOLES in a big red circle with a slash through it. I was still a registered guest, so the bartender only asked what we'd like instead of kicking us out.

I said, "Why would she call? She knows I have a girlfriend."

Mal munched on pretzel sticks. He nodded quickly, his topknot bouncing forward and back. "You got nothing to worry about, man. Unless you want to worry. Do you?"

"What do you mean?"

"I mean, you say you've got a great thing with Hiko, but you gave that girl your number. Could be you want the worry."

"I don't know why I gave it to her."

He ordered another round and nodded again. "Yeah, and that's the bitch. You got to worry about whether or not you wanted to worry."

The bartender brought us two fresh beers and I waited for him to get safely to the bar's other end before continuing. Despite the darkness and desertion of the bar, I couldn't help having a feeling of being watched.

"Should I tell Hiko?"

I expected him to say not to. Instead he shrugged and said, "You should have stood your ground the moment she began to treat you like Darla. You don't have much of a say in what goes on in the house, do you?"

I didn't know what he meant.

Mal drank half his beer, burped loudly, and smiled at me. His wheels spun a moment. "You've got to figure out what you want."

We were both going to pretend that he hadn't mentioned Darla. "I don't know what I want."

"Man, even not knowing something is a kind of knowing. I mean, all the most important stuff you do no one knows about but you. All your decisions and the little debates you have with yourself. That's where your life takes place. The real stuff happens while you're waiting for the subway, choosing what you're gonna do for the rest of your life. Sometimes these moments are shared with one or two others, but mostly it's just you and you. So you go home and you debate this over with yourself, and when you don't come to a conclusion, then you know."

"Know what?"

"That you're fucked. You're not even sure of who you are, let alone what you want." He gulped from his beer and avoided looking at me as he continued. "Before you and I had our falling-out in Redbach's bar, I used to have debates like that every night."

I stirred the foam of my beer with my index finger and wondered what the hell Mal was talking about. I realized that I was seeking advice from a bridge jumper when he said, "Besides, she probably won't even call."

"No, I bet she won't." My stomach loosened up a bit and I rewarded it with a large sip of my beer.

Mal waited for me to put the glass down. "Or maybe she will." He pretended to ignore my squirm as he ordered another.

The next day my internal debate continued. I kept myself near Hiko in the speculative belief that her presence would help me come to a conclusion. I even asked her to go to Michael's office with me. He wanted to go over an offer from a production company about my story. When I asked him, "What story?" he just laughed. I told Hiko that we could go out to dinner after my meeting. She agreed and I called a car service to come pick us up.

In the car she took my hand and asked if I thought

it a good idea to sell my story to a production company when I didn't even know my whole story. "You don't even really know where you came from."

"I know. I will eventually." I watched cars promise collisions if we so much as dared to override our lane. "I hope."

She squeezed my hand and leaned against me. I smelled her citrus-scented shampoo. "I just worry that if nothing turns up, or if you don't like what is found, you'll be crushed."

I stroked her hand. I had never shared any of the research Michael forwarded. Until I saw something that bore some resemblance to me I saw no reason to, and the idea of describing these nonhistories to her made me dizzy. I'd rather just wait until something solid turned up and then share that. I said, "Michael's hired a private investigator. He'll find something."

We hit the bridge and before Hiko could say any more I started to describe the view, how I could see the Statue of Liberty and that the Staten Island Ferry chugged by. I didn't tell her when we passed the gap in the fence where Mal had leaped from the bridge, followed soon by the spot where I had run into a girder and split my head. I thought I recognized that spot just as a B train erupted into view, chasing along beside the flow of cars.

At Michael's office I led Hiko to a sofa in the waiting room. She sat facing a coffee table covered in magazines. I kissed her on the cheek and told her I'd be right back. She refused to let go of my hand.

"Don't you think it's a little silly, signing your life away? You're going to be at their beck and call."

"Right now I don't have any control or money. If I sign this, I get money. One out of two."

"You don't need it that bad."

"Who paid for the cab ride over here?"

She let go of my hand.

Hiko stayed in the waiting area while I went with Michael to discuss the contract. Michael started the meeting by showing me proofs of the photos with Emilia. With Hiko no longer at my side I fell back into a meditation on what Emilia offered. The photos were beautiful: a spectacular shine glinted off the nailheads in the bat and my black eyes, and the hastily done stitches nearly bled in each frame.

Michael smiled across the table at me. "You did good. They loved you. They can't wait for the issue to come out."

I kept looking at the way Emilia's skin melted from the leather outfit and lion's mane. Michael watched my eyes and said, "She had a good time too."

From that point I became too distracted to follow Michael's description of what the movie production company wanted from me. They promised a steady income and some sort of percentage for the rights to my story, whatever it might be, whatever that might mean. Emilia's arched back kept interrupting my focus. All I really got out of our meeting were a couple of repeated words such as *standard clause* and *indemnity*. Michael stood near his large window with a copy of the contract and, when he flipped to a new page, I did the same, pretending to follow along. Behind him, across the square rose a building under construction. A giant crane stabbed up into the air, and from it tons of metal hung quietly, suspended by cables, waiting to be turned into something.

After seven pages of the contract I said, "Let's just get to the heart of it. If I sign, I get some money, right?"

Michael raised his eyebrows at me and said yes.

"And the production company gets the rights to my life story, whatever it may be."

Again Michael said yes.

"And you think this is a fair deal?"

He said he did.

"Where do I sign?"

When I found my way back to Hiko in the waiting room, I discovered her reading a *Vogue* magazine with Emilia on the cover. She kept her head lowered as if concentrating, cocked to one side. She had her sunglasses on.

Everything in our cupboards was labeled with stickers with bumps, even shelf edges. We spent Sundays shopping and Mondays we labeled everything so she could read them. Cans were bumped with *tomato soup*, *chicken noodle*, *broth*. But here she sat, reading a magazine. What if she wasn't really blind at all? Would it make her something else?

What would that make her?

I walked toward her and as I got closer I saw that she had the magazine open with a Braille book inside it. I said, "What are you doing?"

She just barely jumped, but I could see the fear behind the placid face. She looked away from the book. Her fingers played along the center of a page, soaked up the information. "I didn't want to be disturbed, so I pretended I can see. No one asks about Braille when they can't see it."

"Okay. But there's no one else here."

She blushed. "With this thick carpet in here it's hard for me to know when someone is nearby or not."

I put the magazine back on the table for her and took her arm as she stood. When we got to the door, she said, "What's strange is, the book I was reading seemed to be missing some pages."

The next day I left early and stayed out all day. Not knowing what else to do, I went into Manhattan and found a cinemaplex with over ten theaters. I bought a ticket for the next show to start and spent the day wandering from theater to theater. I dragged a giant tub of popcorn and large soda around. I saw parts of the four movies on my floor, none of them very good, and I hardly understood much of any of them. At times I forgot which theater I was in and waited for characters from a different movie to wander into a scene. At moments Michael's research even leaked in and I wondered if that might be the actor who disappeared, or if the story was based on one of the fakirs or accident victims. I started to feel as if all the movies were as connected to me as the research had been, as if somehow I would walk onto the screen and I would both sit in an uncomfortable seat with my feet stuck to a gummy floor and watch myself stack bags against a coming flood, prepare to battle robots from the future, fall in love with the older female teacher across the hall, vanquish demons using ancient powers locked in the heart of a chiseled rock. None of these stories was mine. They might as well have been.

When all the salt and sugar finally had their way with me I left to get real food. I ate half a sandwich in a coffee shop and then browsed through stores near the movie theater. I wandered aisles of CDs, DVDs, and books. Displays at the ends of aisles promised me the greatest entertainment of my life until I reached other displays promising even more.

Michael had given me a thousand-dollar loan from his office petty cash. I started to fill my arms with DVDs and CDs. I avoided books since Hiko already had so many. Hiko's, Braille or not, were enough, and I might read some of them one day. I didn't know how to read Braille but figured that if I ever wanted to badly enough, Hiko could teach me.

With such a wide assortment to choose from I lost track of where I was in the store. The sections all looked the same, bled into one another, overlapped. Occasionally I'd see a name that would pop out at me and I'd recognize it, having heard it from the Brailled-over television in Hiko's living room, or seen it along the side of a city bus, on a billboard, squeezed into place around the headlines of *People*, *Us*, and other less reputable publications. Album covers like artifacts, hieroglyphs depicting the hunt for power and prestige and pagan rights; a young girl dressed like an oversexed woman, a group of young men on a cover sticky with bright pink CLASSIC stickers from an album completed before one or more members overdosed, were committed, or died. I scooped them up. I tried to buy a sense of familiarity. I had nothing at Hiko's of my own. I bought mine.

By the end of the week I was sweating constantly, worried Emilia would or would not call. She'd said she would be in LA for a week and would call when she returned. That week passed. I spent the last two days taking showers and finding reasons not to go out so that I would be there if the phone rang. I stalked around the apartment, carrying the cordless phone while berating myself for not charging it and trying to keep Hiko from thinking I was hiding something as I hid and took the phone with me. I listened to DVDs on my Braille-vision television. I now had a credit card, thanks to Michael, and had wasted no time going to the nearest electronics store and getting everything that my papered-over set needed to be a complete entertainment system. The surround sound drove Hiko out of the room.

"How can you listen to it that loud?"

"It's the only way to get the full experience." I lay on the sofa staring at the ceiling as conversations and sound effects swirled around us. Hiko withdrew into her studio, leaving me with a kiss on my sweaty upper lip.

I began to suffer from headaches that wouldn't end. My stomach tightened but I refused to eat. I was too nervous.

After not eating for a day and a half, hunger finally overrode my concerns about Emilia's call. I'd avoided any contact with Hiko for nearly twenty hours straight and I'd gained some calm. I was famished and, with the phone tucked under my arm, headed into the kitchen to scavenge. I worked on half a chicken that I found in the back of the fridge. Hiko found me kneeling before the fridge with grease and herbs smeared across both cheeks, refrigerator door standing open, bones sprinkled like runes. I grunted as I tore the meat off a thigh. Half-eaten chicken lay on the floor at my knees, along with the foil it had been wrapped in.

Hiko bumped into me as she felt her way to the kitchen sink. "What are you doing down there?" She washed her hands and dried them with a paper towel.

"Eating chicken."

"Isn't that old?"

"Yeah, but it's good."

"Enjoy." She said something about being out of hand soap in the bathroom and shuffled past me.

I had noticed our life together had run low on a lot of

little pieces. Hand soap in the bathroom. Ingredients in the kitchen. Places to put my things. I built a fort out of my large CD and DVD collection. I left stacks of disks in and around the living room. The arms of the sofa were covered with DVDs I'd bought with the advance Michael had gotten me from the production company.

I dumped the chicken carcass into the garbage and headed to the bathroom to brush chicken from my teeth and to dry my hair, still wet from my last shower. With all the showers and sweat over the last two days, it had hardly been dry. Hiko was right, there was no hand soap, and in an act of rebellion I wiped my chicken-coated hands and mouth on the hand towel. I held the phone tightly in my left hand as I angled the hair dryer around my head with my right.

That was when the first swell of nausea rose in me. A second and third wave crashed between my navel and rib cage quickly and, as I watched myself in the mirror, my skin lightened from its normal tone to ash and then green. My eyes looked darker than usual. I felt myself sway with the next curl of my stomach and realized in the moment that I clicked off the dryer that the chicken had been older than it had been tasty. And then the phone rang. Not the cordless I held in my hand, but the hall phone. I had intended to answer the second it rang, so Hiko wouldn't get to the hall phone in time, but now I knew that the battery in the cordless had long been dead. For two days I'd carried around the equivalent of a child's toy. I might as well have carried around the chicken carcass.

I swayed toward the bathroom door, prepared to lurch down the hall and yank the phone from the wall, but then my lunch made its return as a wet and chunky burp, and I turned to the toilet instead. Hands on the bowl, feet planted firmly by the tub, I heaved into an inverted V. I screamed my too-old half chicken into the toilet, light meat, dark meat, crispy skin, fatty yellow globules that I didn't remember going down. I had borrowed this meal for such a short time. I thought, *This is what a mama bird tastes, feeding her young.* Then I screamed some more out, eyes clenched shut, tears streaming up my forehead, acidic burn creeping down the back of my nose. I finally dropped to my knees and cowered before the toilet. I spit and blew chicken from my nose, then rose, not bothering to flush, and guided myself with one hand on the wall, out the door to the hall where I could see Hiko on the phone, smiling and laughing.

"Yes," she said. "That will be nice."

"Who is it?" I asked.

"He sounds like he feels better. I think it was something he ate." She laughed some more. "Okay. Goodbye." She hung up the phone and said, "Are you all right?"

"I'm fine." Vomit dripped off my chin. "Who was that?"

"That was the model you worked with. Emilia. She

is very funny. We are meeting her for coffee tomorrow. Unless you don't feel good."

I dropped my phone.

WE MET EMILIA in a coffee shop near Union Square. On the way I quizzed Hiko over and over about what the conversation had entailed, why she had agreed to meet this woman.

"She said she enjoyed working with you and that she doesn't have many friends in New York." The way Hiko defended this as charity for Emilia let me know it was charity for me. She thought I had too few friends, that I was lonely, that I needed to get out, find something to be other than a pincushion. I couldn't argue, not without revealing that I knew what she thought and that Emilia had lied, that Emilia flaunted my deceitful interest in her, that it was a test of me and my commitment and intentions, that I was failing.

When we entered we found her near the cafe counter, stunning in a black turtleneck, leather jacket, and short red skirt. I held Hiko's arm at the elbow, steered her across the room, past empty tables. As Hiko and I approached, Emilia waved and winked at me with a large grin. Breathing became difficult as Emilia introduced herself to Hiko. "It was so nice talking to you yesterday." She guided Hiko to a nearby table.

Emilia, Hiko, and I sat down, the table so small all three of us were pressed together shoulder to shoulder to shoulder. Our knees bumped under the table. I could feel Emilia's bare skin as she made room for me to slide in.

"You must be very beautiful to be a working model," Hiko said. "The photos of you and Numb must be striking."

"They do a lot of touch-ups." Emilia winked at me as she said this. "Lots of makeup, special lights, lenses."

"Don't be modest," Hiko said.

"She is very pretty," I said. Emilia was. Especially now, in the low light of the coffee shop, her hair pulled back, and wearing deep red lipstick but no other makeup.

A tingle ran up my spine when Hiko said, "May I touch your face?"

"Of course," Emilia said. She leaned forward, eyes on me, and as Hiko reached out Emilia took her hands and pulled them to her face. Softly Hiko touched her cheeks, her forehead, the soft dip of her chin beneath her full bottom lip.

Something shifted on my leg. Emilia's hand rested on my thigh. She stared at me as Hiko examined her face.

Hiko said, "He didn't tell me you were this beautiful. The proportions of your face are perfect." She cupped Emilia's chin. Beneath the table Emilia squeezed my thigh, ran her fingers toward my waist, then she reached up to my face. As Hiko pulled her hands away Emilia dug her nails into the back of my neck. There was intense pressure, then a rush of warmth that trickled down my back.

Emilia pulled her hand away and wiped at her nails. "It's nice to be able to get together with both of you. I don't know many people in the city. I do so much traveling." She spoke warmly and directly to Hiko. She turned in her seat so that I could see along her legs up toward her skirt, which she pulled back a bit. I thought I would melt when she picked up a fork from her plate and touched it, softly at first, against the soft skin of her inner thigh. I looked past Hiko to the clerk oblivious to the sideshow act about to be performed at the too-small table by the window.

"Did he tell you about the photos?"

Behind her glasses, Hiko blinked rapidly. She'd been asking me about them for a week. I'd refused to talk about it. She said, "Not too much, no."

"It's hard to know how to describe them," I said. My eyes were locked on the tines of the fork, at the dimpling they created in Emilia's leg. She dragged it along for a few inches, left four red scratches in her skin. I wanted to be the fork. I also wanted to be that skin.

"I think the photos and interview will be great for you," Emilia said to me. "You won't be surprised when he's famous, will you, Hiko?"

"Of course not. He's a hound for the publicity anyway." She smiled and turned her head toward me. I knew that beneath her cat's-eye sunglasses her black eyes were like painted windows. But still, for a second I thought she saw everything. "You should have heard the way he reacted to a group of fans on the way over here," she said. "They must have seen the film of him with the lion."

"Whether I want to be famous or not, I may not have a choice," I said at last. My hand trembled as I reached out. "If the contract I signed leads to anything, I'll just have to deal with it, be a part of whatever they cook up."

"Why?" Hiko asked.

"I don't want some idiot playing me."

Emilia laughed. "You should let them do whatever the hell they want. Take the money and run."

"It isn't that simple."

"Of course it is. If you don't remember any of your past anyway, why feel tied to it? Cut the cord, take their money, and don't look back."

I touched Emilia's thigh. She took my hand and guided it to the scratches left by the fork. We sat like that for just under an hour, Hiko's sightless eyes watching Emilia guide my fingers along the lines she'd gouged into her skin, my hand becoming warm and then hot as I felt the small ridges, raised and red and probably sore, parallel and barely separated and ruining the perfect white of her thigh. We spoke of her travel. We spoke of Hiko's art. I thought of where else a fork might go.

Emilia said, "I have to go soon, but maybe you could walk me back to my place?"

Hiko smiled. "We'd love to. It's a nice day for a walk."

Emilia pressed my hand against her leg and said, "Yes, and then you'll know where I live. You can drop by anytime."

With my free hand I reached to the back of my neck and felt the small oozing scratch that Emilia had left there.

I said, "So, let's get going then." I helped Hiko out of her seat and the three of us walked out of the coffee shop, me between the two women, guiding the blind one by the arm and tightly gripping the other's hand.

THE FIRST TIME I went to Emilia's apartment alone I forced myself to think of it as a casual, friendly visit. My self-delusion lasted until I knocked on her door and she answered it in only a pair of jogging shorts.

All she said at the door was, "Finally."

She took me into her living room. Overwhelming deep red walls backed the burgundy leather couch, which swallowed me as I sank into it. She grabbed my belt and said, "You're going to show me that scar this time."

As she undid my belt, I looked at the light on the ceiling. When Hiko and I had walked her back here, we had parted at the street with Emilia giving both me and Hiko warm hugs and an invitation to visit. Now I lay on my back as she pulled my pants to my ankles. Her ceiling light looked like a giant eyeball. It stared right back at me and never blinked.

She dug her nails into my thigh, raising red lines alongside the old white scar. "It's so pretty," she said. She kissed the scar and began to lick it. I swore her tongue had a cat's roughness as she lapped at the scar and the red welts she'd raised. She was absorbed by it. Her hands clung to my thigh and calf; she climbed me like a tree. She pushed her mouth against my leg and my flesh twitched beneath her. I began to pet her head.

She stopped and said, "Your skin is so soft." She gave the scar another kiss.

We didn't talk much more than that, and I only stayed for an hour. She left me with a large purple hickey over my scar. At the door I noticed that her living room and hallway were lined with etchings and drawings of people in distorted, tortured poses.

"What are these?"

"I collect depictions of the saints. Those tortured for their love of God."

"Are you very religious?"

She laughed, her arms cradled over her bare chest, goose bumps rising in the cool fall air. "God, no."

I left her apartment and started to wander. I called Mal and told him what happened.

"I'm not sure what I'm supposed to tell you, buddy." In the background behind him I could hear yelling and hip-hop music. He named a club uptown. "Come find us and we can talk."

When I got there, he was sitting with Karen in the corner. In the poorly lit room I didn't think it was her at first, perhaps trying to project onto Mal the same sort of infidelity I had committed, but when she stood up and I saw how high her platform shoes were I recognized her. Each of us took turns buying rounds.

When Mal went to the restroom, Karen and I found ourselves dipped in an awkward silence. She avoided eye contact for a minute, then smiled at me.

"Mal tells me you've got a big contract working? Development deal of some sort?"

"Something like that."

"Will it be here or in LA?"

"Both, I guess. It depends on the company's expectations."

She nodded. "Depends on what you do, I guess."

"Yeah, I guess."

"Mal did some time in LA."

I hadn't known that. "When?"

"After you moved into the Thomas. He took off not too long after."

Mal stopped off at the bar before returning to the table, and when he brought back another round Karen asked him about his time in LA. His jaw muscles tightened. "Not much to tell." His lie fell flat at our feet and Karen stepped on it and kicked it toward the next table.

Karen hit his arm. "That's bullshit. What about your accident?" To me: "He stayed with some guy who sold weed to make money, and he borrowed the dealer's car—"

Mal waved his hand to cut her off. "My time there was a waste. I couldn't get any work. Then I read about an upcoming gig at an MTV concert. They had posters all over the beach advertising this thing that was going to have all sorts of sideshow stuff. So, I figured I'd do some fireballs and make a few bucks.

"I'm on my way there in that drug dealer's piece-of-shit BMW when suddenly the engine screeches like it's been stabbed and the brakes fail. Last I remembered there wasn't a car near me, so I try to get to the right shoulder. Out of nowhere there's this car. I hit it, ricochet back the other way, and hit a barricade. Someone pulled me out of the car. I had fire-eating shit in the trunk; it exploded. It was bad, I guess. Don't remember."

He gripped his mug so tight I thought it might shatter. He continued. "Fire truck shows up, ambulance, police. Ten stitches across my chin and a broken jaw. It pretty much sucked."

He never said that he blamed me for the accident. He rubbed his hands across the rough table edge, his thumbs pressed down to white. He looked away, and as the light from the neon sign behind him struck his face I said, "I think I see the scar."

"No, you don't." I don't know why he said that. I could

see it, just a small stripe slightly shining under his beard. *I can see it,* I thought.

Karen grabbed his chin and turned his head to face her. "That accident brought you back for me to find." She kissed him gently and touched his hair. "He was on painkillers for months. He still suffers from pain in his neck and jaw when the weather changes."

Mal's eyes bore into the table. A quiet minute, then he looked at me and said, "So that was what I learned about LA. Never drive a drug dealer's car." His forced laugh didn't hide the pain in his eyes.

ten

AT FIRST, WHEN I arrived at the Thomas' lobby, I didn't see Mal. Then I saw his topknot over the back of a tall leather chair. He was reading a *Playboy* and drinking a cup of coffee.

"Hey, man." He grinned up at me.

"Why'd you want to meet here?"

He puffed out his bottom lip. "You're no fun. How long did you live here? Six months? I figured you'd want to get back to your roots."

"My roots."

"Hey, man, you want to go back to the St. Mark's, we can do that. But that's not where it happened for you. It started here, right? The big contract. Money pouring in. Congrats and all that." He poured his coffee in the planter next to the chair and rolled up the magazine. He started talking through it like a megaphone.

"This man is famous. This man has been on TV." Embarrassed, I told him to shut up.

Faces behind the desk pretended not to hear us. Because I had been a tenant for six months, their patience ran longer for me than for others. The lounge area was a large room with low, overstuffed leather furniture and low, wide lamps that barely cast any light. The walls were covered in a mural depicting the story of Noah's ark. Animals mated in twos marched around the room's perimeter until they finally reached Noah's big boat, which sat in rising water above the wide entrance of the room. Across the ceiling, beams arched up above us like the belly of an upside-down boat. I knew it illustrated a Bible story, but as Mal barked through the rolled-up magazine and other guests turned and looked at us, it turned into a mural of the circus I'd run away from. And the arched ceiling changed from a boat to a circus tent, and the groups of hotel guests, in their suits and fine dresses, seemed like my audiences, there to see the man in scars and jeans who worked with hammers and nails but no wood.

I grabbed Mal's arm but he continued to shout invitations at guests through the magazine, sprinkling in creative obscenities, until I pushed him through the revolving door leading onto 47th Street. When I followed him through, he stood on the curb and laughed.

I walked toward Times Square. "Always trying to get attention, aren't you?"

He stopped laughing and fell into step beside me. "And you've always got it, don't you? I've seen a lot of you lately."

"The magazine?"

"Not just that. You've been on television too. And not just the Caesar tape. Apparently they got tired of that one. There are other films of you. Or at least it looks like you. You at a bank getting hit by the revolving door."

"Turned out later that I broke my thumb."

"Yeah, well, they don't go into that. Then there's the *Late Show* gig, with the nail chair. And you getting hit by a bus. In all of these short films you hobble along, unaware of any injury. There's just so many of them I wonder if they can all be you."

"What do you mean?"

"I mean, what's the deal with that contract you signed? Hiko told Karen what she knew. It sounded like anything that's public knowledge is owned by the production company."

"Yeah, so?"

"So what if you're being followed? What if someone's setting you up for these accidents?"

He stopped and we both turned slowly, eyes leading where our faces, grim, paranoid, followed, until we both had revolved in a circle, in opposite directions, looking for who or what, I didn't know. Most likely a small man with a camera crew, a tall director's chair, and a megaphone, real, not misused pornography, ready to yell "Roll!" at the first hint that I might break my arm or trip into an oncoming hansom cab. When neither of us saw anything Mal grabbed my arm and pulled me forward again.

I said, "You're crazy. Why would they set me up? I get into enough stuff on my own."

"Not enough for a movie or television. Not enough to hold the public's attention. If you knew about your past, you might have enough there, but, well, you don't."

Somewhere, I knew, Michael continued his research. If he didn't find anything, if nothing ever turned up, then . . . what, exactly? Would I be plagued by short films from bank security cameras and (un)lucky tourists with camera phones? More than ever I wanted my sight to turn inward, to look back through my own mind and see into what I was before I wandered through the dust and desert winds into Tilly's arms. Just one hint, one item of what I might be to anchor myself, to throw to Michael and the movie producers, like horse meat for a lion.

We were on Broadway now, fighting our way upstream against a surge of tourists and theatergoers. We stopped and watched a cowboy in his underwear play guitar.

Mal asked, "What are you going to do about it?" "It" being my lack of control, my having signed away any and all rights without thinking it through, my stupidity, my life. "It," as always, being limited to nothing and able to slip between the spaces from one of my failures to the next. "It" was long overdue for fixing.

"I don't know."

"Wow." Mal shook his head and walked away from the audience surrounding the underwear cowboy.

I followed after him. He ducked through the crowd with his arms stretched to either side, as if surfing. He had little trouble getting through the people. I tripped twice as I tried to catch up, smashed into a woman's shopping bag, felt something crunch and kept going.

"What should I do?" I shouted.

He answered over his shoulder. "Do anything. Run away. Buy your own camera and film yourself all day and night to make sure you know what's true and what's bullshit. Sue them. Just do something."

He crossed the street to the lane divider cutting Broadway in half. He stood at the center, traffic speeding by on either side of him, waiting for me. When the cars let up, I ran out to him.

He stuffed his hands in his pockets. "You are just like you were in the circus. So friggin' passive. Take some control, for God's sake."

I realized this was what he hadn't been able to say before, when I was nailed to Redbach's bar. I thought he'd learned something while we had been out of touch. He had learned how to protect himself without hurting others. My friend was back. This was the man who had tried to save me from a lion, not the man who tried to wake me up by nailing me to a bar. He'd learned how to take care of himself and others, I thought. I counted myself lucky. I didn't know how wrong I was.

I said, "Not everyone knows what they want, Mal."

"Yeah, but anyone can take a little control until they figure it out. For instance, what are you doing about that chick who's after you? Did you tell Hiko you're leaving?"

He knew I hadn't.

"You haven't, and you haven't told that model to leave you alone either. You're still sleeping with her, aren't you?"

I blushed and he laughed at me.

"You told me you don't even really like her. Do you know why you're doing her? Because she wants you to. Not because you want to, but because she wants you to. Just like when you moved in with Hiko, probably. Just like when I brought you to New York. You've never said no to anyone."

"Well, what's so great about your life? You're living with a weird woman in a tiny little studio, with no job, and you look like hell."

"What's great about my life is I say no all the time, man. I've chosen a hard path, but it's the one I chose. Did you know that Michael tried to recruit me after you signed with him? Wanted to get you a sidekick, he said."

"You're not my sidekick."

He laughed. "Shut the hell up. I *was*. I was your frig-gin' assistant. I held the nail, for Christ's sake." The smile fell off his face. "But I told him to go screw himself and that was the moment I realized I was angry at *you* for what *I* was doing. I decided to take some of your energy for myself. That's what the jump's about."

I didn't understand. "How did the jump help?"

Mal checked out the traffic in both directions. "No, not the one you went to. Another jump. A bigger jump. I'll call you when we're ready for it. You'll have a bit part in the story that is me." He flashed a smile and jumped into the uptown lane of traffic. A bus rumbled toward us and he moved to the dotted line dividing the two northbound lanes. He turned and raised his hands and yelled, "You can be my sidekick," as the bus moved between us. When it pulled past he had vanished. As the bus continued uptown, I could see Mal running alongside, jogging to keep pace with it as it struggled through the heavy traffic. It was a simple and ultimately ineffective disappearing act. I lost track of him in the traffic lights and the passing taxis and I wondered if Michael would have wanted me if Mal had been the one with the great "talent" that drew attention.

When I got home I found Hiko soaking in a warm bath.

She greeted me with a kiss and a question. "Where have you been?"

"With Mal."

I sat on the edge of the tub. She soaked navel deep. Steam coated the tiles and mirror with a film of condensation. I slid down to the floor by the tub, watching her soap her arms, rinse them off.

"Karen is really happy you and Mal have become friends again."

"Really?"

"Yeah, she thinks you are a good influence on him."

I watched her large dark eyes as she said this, but I didn't see any hint of irony, so I let it go. I breathed in the soapy air and felt safe in the white room. "It's like heaven in here," I said.

Hiko smiled and her eyes cast about the room, not finding me.

EMILIA AND I began to meet at her place more frequently, finally climaxing with three visits on the same day, a Thursday.

At first she would welcome me at the door of her apartment, the little peephole darkening under her eye only the first two times. By the end she was answering the door naked, making me wonder if there weren't other men or women in her life who shared this welcome, if there was a UPS driver or bike messenger, a super for the building, butt crack yawning between blue jeans and tool belt, who knocked in a way similar to me. I began to work on a secret knock in my head, one I planned to share but never did. I worried that someone else would get the greeting meant for me. What if someone else knocked and then checked their watch, and as the door latch clicked and the flesh-colored door pulled back they looked down, past the roaring second hand of their Timex, and then moved up along the long bare toes, the curve of the ankle, up over the muscular calf, up the thigh, the furred thong, specially made for my visits to "Caesar's den," as we called it, with a special split crotch and a three-foot tail in the back, a little puff of actual lion's mane on the end, and the delicious rivet of her navel, the abdomen, still red from my nails (nails and nails), and up to the breasts, rising and falling with heavy, possibly embarrassed breath, and along her neck, the ruby lips pursed in a surprised little O, wide eyes all but saying, *I thought it was someone else, and now I'm all naked,* in a singsongy little-girl falsetto. At this sight the milkman, postman, UPS, super, plumber, one or all of these, who knows, whispers, "I tawt I taw a putty-tat." With Tweety's innocent blink he steps forward and the two begin to re-enact Warner Brothers' most sexually charged animated teams, consuming each other, a sadomasochistic game that was supposed to be mine alone.

My time with Emilia was always exhausting. After we'd finish tearing each other's flesh as foreplay, I'd lie back and she'd go to work on me. Once we extinguished our drives with what she called "traditional" positions, Emilia would roll off me and I'd stare at the ceiling. After about six weeks of this we'd fallen into as much of a pattern as I had with Hiko. No longer dangerous or exciting, it was my life.

On the other hand, Hiko and I would go to a gallery or a museum or a showing of her friends' work. Amid drinks and small reheated appetizers we would hold hands and wander. Those shows or pieces that allowed Hiko to feel the work were, of course, more interesting for her. Otherwise it was just an opportunity to network. We'd eventually wander home with some sort of late-night takeout or we'd pick up ingredients for something we'd make ourselves. We'd end up in bed, holding each other or not, falling asleep almost immediately.

I had stopped telling Hiko any sort of excuse for my leaving. At the beginning I'd say something about shopping or Mal or even just a walk. Now I just said, "Be back later."

Late one afternoon I found Emilia's front door standing open and as I came in Emilia called to me from the bedroom. I walked down the dark hallway and found her sitting quietly on the bed—in a black sweater and jeans.

I'd already scripted out in my head what I would say, but before I said, *Emilia, I've been thinking*, she had both removed my belt and tied me to the bed with it. This sounds more complicated than it was. One moment I was standing, looking at her thick glasses, and the next I was saying, "Make it tighter, I can still get loose." I thought I heard a clasp close as she connected me, rack style, to the king-sized bed, too large for the room.

She left me there and went into the living room. When she came back in she wore the lion bikini.

"I had an inspiration," she said.

"I guessed that." I thought she meant belting me to the bed until she showed me her new gloves. She held them in front of me and flexed her fingers. Out of the furry paws poked long, curved claws.

"Those look real."

"They are," she said.

"They're so big." I imagined the age of the lion that they had been pulled from. Some old king.

"The better to tear you to pieces with."

"That's not a lion in that story. I think it's a wolf."

"Don't be smart, or you won't make it home tonight."

I was already erect. She slipped backward onto me and as she sat back she put her paws onto my shoulders and dug her claws into me. What had started with pinches and scratches and a lion bikini ended with stainless-steel forks, safety pins, and a plastic-covered mattress. Blood ran off me onto her sheets as she scratched me down the chest, into my ribs. She dug the claws deep into me around my waist. She proved more creative that evening than she had been in weeks, asking me to do things I'd never done, and doing things I hadn't known I'd like.

"I like the love handles," she said. "Something to hold." She smiled her claws in deeper. I was dizzy. She did what she wanted to me and I stared over her shoulders. Strangely, I noticed that all her pictures and the mirror were off the walls, and the curtains were gone. The windows were bare and black and reflected the lights of the room back at me. Other than the bed, it was a nearly empty room.

By the time we finished, she had clawed four 3-inch valleys into each of my sides and nearly removed a large patch of skin from my back. It hung like a torn pocket. We spent a few minutes playing with hydrogen peroxide and then she started eating chocolate chip ice cream.

"I gotta turn in," she said. She set the ice cream on the nightstand and started to strip the bed. The bloody sheets were balled up and thrown on the floor. "I'll talk to you tomorrow." She smiled and turned away as she prepared to remake the bed.

As I tucked my shirt in I remembered the reason I'd gone to her place. "Emilia, I wanted to talk to you about our relationship."

She snapped a clean sheet over the bed and smoothed it with her palms. Her face was hidden by her hair. "Oh, yeah. I wanted to mention to you. I'm moving to Los Angeles."

I stood frozen, one shoe in my hand, stooped forward looking for the other one I no longer cared to find. When the word *moving* left her lips my eyes had locked onto the bloody sheets balled at my feet. Against the pale yellow of them were tiny black flecks of blood. When I'd gotten there two hours earlier, those flecks had been in me.

"What will you do in LA?"

"I've gotten a part in a movie."

"I thought you were just a model."

She stood up straight, hands on her hips. Her hair covered one eye and the other glared at me. "What does that mean?"

"I don't know." I did know: I'd thought her just a model. She and I had never really talked, never heard each other's plans. We knew nothing of successes or failures. How was I supposed to know that she had any plans beyond piercing me with sharp objects and standing half naked in front of a camera?

She finished making the bed. As she threw the dirty sheets into her closet, she said, "If you ever visit LA, you should look me up." She had ended our relationship. Denial was my best defense. I began my rejection of this fact by remembering that we didn't have a relationship, not in any conventional sense. We had events. Struggling efforts. Cataclysms. So this didn't end any relationship, and if I simply walked away now, I could pretend that no such ending had occurred.

I walked into the other room. "Yeah, definitely. In fact, I think I should visit LA." I found my shoe in the hallway but didn't put it on until I stood in the elevator, halfway to the lobby.

I imagined Emilia in her room, relieved that I hadn't pressed staying together or breaking up. She was like me, I thought, totally screwed up to the point of uncertainty about everything.

That evening, Mal dropped by Hiko's brownstone unexpectedly. He had a brown box of gear that held some of the jump equipment. He asked me to hold on to it for him.

"I'll be back in a day or so for it. Karen just doesn't want it around her, so if you could hang on to it . . . ?" I figured he and Karen had fought over the jump.

I took the box and he left after promising to call me the next day. Despite what he said, he didn't call or come back. I knew I would see him because I had his harness. I went through his gear, pulled out the harness and left the rope, clasps, and unopened bundles of gauze in the box. There were six old mayonnaise jars filled with a jelly mixture that smelled like gasoline. I feared the odor alone might strip paint off the walls. I tightened the lids carefully and put the box in the back courtyard in a sealed cooler. Something told me to bury it.

I tried to put the harness on but couldn't figure out the right way to wear it. After a while I half convinced myself it wasn't even the same bungee harness. I hung it on the back of a living room chair. It clung there, like a pet spider, sprawled out, territorial. It scared me. I gave it a wide berth, kept my distance as if it might leap at me. The room had only one other place to sit, the sofa, and I'd covered it in DVDs and CDs and magazines I wasn't reading, so I had no place to go to. I began to think of it as Mal's room. Soon the harness gave me the impression Mal hid in the room, lurking in a corner, behind furniture, perhaps even browsing through books in Braille. I stopped using the front of the apartment. I didn't disturb it. I didn't play music. I didn't touch the TV. I didn't turn on the lights.

Several nights after Mal dropped the box off I sat in the kitchen, pretending to read some new reports Michael had sent me. They'd sat on the kitchen table for weeks, some of them months, as I'd worked hard to ignore them. Fewer had come lately, mostly thin, single-page notes. The envelopes were thicker the farther down the pile I worked. The older the envelope, the more it held. I tired of reading them, the tales with no ending, only beginnings that all sounded the same, with disturbed young men, histories of mental illness, disappearances, accidents, poorly copied photos, or photos clear enough that the men were obviously not me. They'd all taken on the same sad quality. Layered in with the reports were scripts from the production company, suggestions of how I might be used in a Will Ferrell vehicle or a Farrelly brothers picture. The scripts, like the reports, all sounded the same, and I flipped through them quickly, eyes wandering, always to the same place, down the hall to the living room where the chair sat with the harness draped on its back.

The metal clasps and hooks winked at me from down the hall. The danger they represented crept out into the city; it leaked from Hiko's home, and I decided I should leave town. Emilia would be going to California. I could get there first. I called Michael with my last-minute decision that I needed to go to Hollywood. I could do a movie, I said.

"What are you talking about?" he said. "You aren't signed for anything."

"A TV show, then."

"Listen, we don't have anything right now. I'll keep you posted. Just stay in New York."

"Is there something you're not telling me?" I asked.

"It's just really quiet right now. Don't panic." In his instruction to not panic I thought I heard his panic. Selling me was proving harder than he'd anticipated.

The next day I still didn't hear from Mal, but I did hear from Karen. She came by just before lunch and Hiko invited her to stay. Hiko left Karen and me alone in the kitchen for a moment. I was cutting turkey breast and Karen sprang on me as soon as Hiko was out of the room.

"Mal's having an affair, isn't he?"

At the word *affair* my hand slipped and the knife slid through the side of my left hand. Blood spilled out of my newest wound and I grabbed a towel.

My guilt about Emilia kept me from looking Karen in the eye as I said, "I really don't think he is."

"He'd tell you, though."

"I don't know. But I don't think he is."

"You don't think. You can find out. Call him and find out."

I no longer even tried to look at her, so I just watched

the blood run from the back of my hand onto the cutting board instead. It calmed me. "I've been waiting for him to call me. When he does—"

"Don't wait. Call him. Call him today."

I could hear Hiko coming back down the hallway. I whispered, "Have you mentioned this to Hiko?"

"She doesn't think he would either. But she's too trusting."

"What does that mean?"

Hiko returned and Karen pulled bread from the cupboard and brought it to me. When she put it down her eyes fell on the cut in my hand. She tore some paper towels from the roll and pressed it against the wound. The small fiber quilting of the towels turned red with blood. Karen's long nails flashed at me. She didn't seem concerned about touching it. I focused on her hand.

She said, "I mean that for some reason she always picks the losing side." She looked up at me, face hard as stone, not a hint of a smile or levity, and then cleaned the knife to cut the bread.

I went into the other room and found my stapler and sealed the wound shut. It was too tight and wouldn't heal well. I didn't care.

I never did call Mal for Karen. Instead, I pretended she hadn't said a thing and I waited for him to call me. He never did, but he showed up at eleven two nights later.

"Tonight's the night. Have you got my stuff?"

I had spent days with his equipment reminding me of our conversation on the street, his hint at a bigger jump, one that would make him the star of the story. I had to know what he meant.

I told Hiko I was going out and we ran out to the cab he'd brought, the cooler between us. The harness jangled from my pocket; the clasps flashed in the headlights of the cab. When we got inside I told him about Karen's suspicions.

Mal shook his head. "She knows something's up but won't believe it's not another woman." On his lap rested the box of gear.

"So she doesn't know about the jump?"

He laughed. "Are you kidding?"

"Does she know about any of this? This gear? What you did before? The test jump?"

He sighed and said, "Sometimes telling people too much is like giving them control over you, like attaching a leash to yourself and handing it to them. Sometimes it's just better to keep some things hidden. You understand that, right?"

I shook my head. I didn't understand, not then, maybe not even later. By way of explanation he whistled and pantomimed an hourglass shape with both hands—the international gesture for a curvaceous female—and I realized he meant Emilia.

I said, "That's completely different."

"Is it? So Hiko wouldn't be mad? She'd be pleased?

Like Karen would be to find out that you've been holding on to bungee gear for me?"

We rode in silence. I stared out the window. Mal checked the gear. We arrived at the bridge and found what I thought was an odd press scene. Fifty people, maybe more, on the bridge. Three had cameras. One, an enormous actual reel-to-reel film camera, knocked into people as the goat-faced adolescent holding it pushed through the crowd to find Mal. A fuzz-faced boy grinning at everyone held a cigarette-box-sized digital video camera. Cell phones flashed everywhere. Last was a boring old camcorder held by a large, slightly pigeon-toed woman whose horn-rimmed glasses reflected the lights of the city. Lenses swung left and right as the individuals filmed the crowd filming the individuals. No one had a light of any kind. I pointed around us and said, "Too bad there's no lights. No way any of these films turn out."

Mal laughed. "Yeah, but this way the cops won't see us."

The crowd started up the bridge. I moved off by myself. After a solemn march we reached the high point of the bridge. Redbach, already stationed at the same spot as before, pulled back the fencing and tied it in place. The wind roared. The last time we'd been there it had turned calm. The wind died down as we came to the apex, but this time Redbach almost looked afraid he'd blow off the bridge. He gripped the rail as he waited for Mal to get ready.

Mal prepared himself in front of the crowd. He put the harness on. With the final strap adjusted, he stood with his arms stretched out and Jerry and Redbach pulled out a heavy gray cloth and began to wrap it around him, as if preparing a mummy. Jerry wrapped his arms and legs first, followed by his chest and stomach.

I walked over to them. “What is that?”

Jerry didn’t stop wrapping. “Fire-retardant wrap.”

Mal watched my eyes as he pulled a tight gray covering over his head. His tall topknot just a bulge underneath, he tucked the strands of loose hair around his face and at his neck under the wrapping. Only his long goatee was visible when he finished. He then smeared what looked like petroleum jelly over his face and into his beard. Someone remarked that it was another fire retardant.

Gray fabric wrapped double-thick, Jerry opened the cooler and began to apply jelly from the mayonnaise jars. Even in the high wind the odor clung to us, threatened to erupt into flame despite the absence of fire. They applied it to his legs and back, with a little on the backs of his arms.

Mal grinned at me and said, “We want fire, but not too much.” His eyes flashed as someone took a picture. At his feet were the coils of the rope and bungee cord. He looked like a jellyfish at the end of a fisherman’s line.

I stepped close to him so only he would hear me. “Mal, is this safe?”

He laughed and raised his arms to allow for more jelly to be painted onto his sides. I couldn't stop him any more than he could have stopped me outside Caesar's cage. I'd have to support him as he'd supported me. "You let me know if you want to leave, and we can just leave."

"That's bullshit and you know it. These people want to see something burn, and I'm it."

Black shadows of metal coils and girders reached out above us, and the main support beams shone in bright spotlights. I suddenly realized that the real centerpiece out here was the bridge. No matter what Mal did, the bridge would remain. The pillars seemed to hold up the sky. Mal would do what he wanted, and, whatever the result, the bridge would remain. Then someone else would try something else, and success or failure, the bridge would remain. Mal was wrong about finding some space to claim as your own. You never claimed any space—it claimed you. Tilly's circus had claimed me, as had Redbach's bar, Hiko's studio, Emilia's bed. I heard Los Angeles calling for its shot at me in the wind coming up the East River.

Mal addressed us, his throng, lackeys and worshippers. "Ladies and gentlemen, I am glad you all came here tonight. Some would say that what I'm about to try is the act of a madman. Others might say it's an act of stupidity. Yet others just want to see a guy set himself on fire. To all of you I say, kiss my ass. But you will have to jump off this bridge to do that."

He climbed onto the rail. Unlike at the previous

jump, I felt him taking the story from me. He wouldn't be forgotten. I would. He would not.

He reached out and called to Redbach. "Scissors." A pair with bright blue handles appeared and in a series of jagged cuts he removed the goatee that reached down to his chest. He held the braids out and handed them to Jerry.

"A keepsake for the lucky lady," someone said, and people laughed.

I could feel it in the crowd. Mal wasn't jumping in as much as we were throwing him off. The crowd demanded it. I almost sensed a cage around us.

A spotlight popped on. It was held by the reel-to-reel operator. The large camera with the great wheel of film clicked away in one hand; in his other a small klieg threw light over Mal.

Somewhere behind us Karen imagined Mal in the heat of an affair. He'd spent time practicing all the steps to this with Jerry and Redbach. She never would have allowed it. He'd hidden everything related to it with me. He'd not been with another woman. He'd been with something that could kill him. She had been wrong on the details, but it had still been an affair.

Redbach lit a torch with his lighter. He stood about ten feet away from Mal, far enough not to light him too soon. Mal faced us, his arms raised. Everyone moved to the rail, fanned out to his left and his right. I stood next to Jerry, almost twenty feet from Mal. Redbach stepped up and touched Mal's boot. Immediately blue flames licked up his legs and, as Redbach yelled, "Go," Mal erupted in a column of orange fire. He jumped off backward and for a moment his arms stayed out at his sides, but then he began to swing them and his legs kicked.

The time I'd seen him jump before, he had disappeared into the darkness beneath the bridge and everyone had been forced to imagine him swinging beneath us, but this time he screamed his way down and, like a comet, he left a phosphene trail in the air behind. He reached the end of his line, began to slow, and finished as a small orange dot that broke the surface of the water and was extinguished. The burning light he had been left grand, sweeping arcs in my vision. I blinked at them and listened to the others. No one knew how to react. A few started to applaud. From the opposite end of the crowd, barely audible, someone said, "Oh God!"

Far below us, swinging slowly, a small fire burned its way up the line. Either the line they used wasn't fireproof or jelly had spilled onto it, but an orange line hung below us like a fuse, and trapped at the end waited Mal. He had dipped under the water for only a few seconds, just long enough to douse the flames, but hanging in the air now, suspended above the river's rolling surface, nothing kept the flames from creeping to him. He reignited into a fireball.

"Motherfucker. He's still on fire," Redbach said. Someone else yelled to cut the line. No one did anything.

People moved away from the rail. The camera continued to click, and Jerry started to scream down to Mal.

Finally able to let go of the rail, I moved to the knotted rope at the buttress. Redbach stood there, staring at the bridge's girders, unsure what to do. I grabbed the rope and shouted, "Help me get him up here."

He looked at me as if just realizing he wasn't alone. "No," Redbach said. "We need to cut him loose. The water will put him out." He searched through the bag at his feet and found a large butterfly knife.

That's when the spotlights from the chopper snapped on. Redbach looked at me and said, "Do we stay?"

I looked over the edge of the rail. Ahead arched the Brooklyn Bridge and beyond it Staten Island and the Statue of Liberty. I looked down. Mal swung into view, then under the bridge, a small, burning match. I saw a reflection of him in the water beneath. Both were struggling.

"Jesus Christ," I said. "He's still burning."

"Yeah," Redbach said. "Jesus Christ." He kept repeating that as he began to cut through the line.

We stood and waited for the police. The chopper swung around in the air, its engine laboring to keep the unflyable shape suspended in the air above us, the pilot clearly working against the high winds and afraid to approach tree-thick bridge cables. Bug-eyed searchlights danced toward us.

"Do they know he's down there?" I said.

"I don't know." Redbach's sweat dripped onto his hands as he got through the last part of the line. He'd cut himself in his efforts and, unfeeling, worked despite it. Blood dropped onto the bridge deck beside his knees. I looked back over the handrail and watched as once more the small orange dot at the end of the line dropped into the water. This time it wasn't moving. He'd stopped his struggle.

Pounding of feet and the lights from police cars. Six or seven uniforms, heavy in the middle, hanging over gun belts, made their way to us. They took turns asking us questions and peering over the edge. One of the cops squinted down at Mal and said, "This guy lit himself on fire and jumped off the bridge?"

"Yeah," Redbach said.

"What a fucking moron," the cop said as he turned away. He shouted into his radio and the chopper swung away from the bridge. Beneath us, lost in the new darkness that had rolled in after Mal's second loss of fire, a police boat circled, small floodlights trained on the lettering on its side. One larger light swept the water ahead and another popped on behind as they looked for my friend.

Redbach and I were arrested and booked for trespassing and disturbing the peace. In the processing station, one of the officers eyed us carefully.

"Hey," he said, "you that guy?" He pointed at the palm of his hand, finger cocked like a pistol, and made a nail gun sound. "You are, ain't you? My kid has downloaded stuff about you off the Web."

"Yeah, that's me."

He stamped a form and wrote something above the smeared red ink. "I couldn't believe that last thing my kid downloaded. That sex tape of yours is sick."

I stood there, not sure what to say. I could feel my back curving as my knees wobbled.

He looked at Redbach. "And you, you're his pal, aren't you? Put the nails in him?"

Redbach turned pale. "No," he said. "Not me."

Another cop walked in as they took our mug shots. Mine is now famous. It ran in *Time* and *Newsweek* and was eventually named one of the fifty most recognizable images of the year. My eyes, swollen half shut from crying, are red, and sweat and tears run down my cheeks. The photo was taken just as the cop said to me and Redbach, "Sorry about your friend. He was DOA."

Redbach and I both became sick in the small plastic wastebasket in the corner behind the police cameraman, who kindly waited for us to finish before saying we could help ourselves to coffee or water before we headed to our cells.

Released from jail the next day, I went to Hiko's apartment and made our home happily devoid of any modern conveniences. God help me if Hiko heard about the film the cop had seen, heard about it on the radio or my television. I had no idea what it was and didn't want to find out. I had also discovered that the videos shot the previous night were being shown on the news. I wanted none of my films to enter my home. I felt them rising outside, like a tide, and I kept expecting to hear thunder and catch flashes of lightning from the corner of my eye, as if the flood of information were a real storm raging outside my window. The cab ride home had been horrific, as the cabbie spent most of the trip, eyes on the mirror, smile on his face, trying to engage me in conversation about the reports rising from his radio. I'd only just escaped his questions about my "talents" and the "tragedy" of my friend. Did self-immolation equal tragedy? Since then the constant radio chatter and television reports from other buildings and cars on the street had pattered on my ears like rain. A storm, a flood.

I circled the living room. The television and electronics equipment sat around me. Some might say, though not me, that I had "earned" them. Mal had deserved more than he'd gotten, had actually worked toward something, however ridiculous, and died. He'd killed himself to get what I had gotten without trying. The electronics, my prizes, buzzed even when turned off, hummed with the need to repeat reports and videos of Mal's death. They dared me to listen. They dared me not to.

I could have sold the equipment, the electronics. Instead, I threw them away. To be more accurate, I threw them out the window. It started with a couple of CDs that I decided would never be listened to again. They had both been Mal's. Out the window.

It felt good, holding them out there and letting gravity do its thing. I sat by the window and dropped one after another of the disks from our metal rack bought at an overpriced, trendy furniture store. After a while I ran out of CDs. What good is a CD player without any CDs? Out the window. DVDs and DVD player followed. The TV proved the bitch of the litter—it just didn't want to fit—but with a tremendous cracking sound part of the window frame gave way and at last it went. I found that there is a beautiful, quiet moment when something falls. The television, like the other items before it, hung there for a second, not appearing to move but instead only getting smaller. It looked as if it might never hit bottom, as if it might just shrink silently to nothing. At last it, as the other appliances had, exploded into a reminder that everything is only a collection of parts, no matter how solid the shell. In this way the items of my life had been shrunk down to nothing, rendered incomplete in their collapse to parthood, parts only now adding up to more refuse instead of useful items. Beneath me, in the back courtyard, about ten feet from where the cooler had sat for weeks with Mal's fire jelly, scattered my exploded life.

As I leaned out the window, looking down, I felt blood on my face and a salty taste in my mouth. Drops fell from my chin and shrank until they splattered below on the television, CDs, and DVDs. I had no idea how I had hurt myself. Cut myself on the window, maybe, or bitten through my lip. It wouldn't be the first time. On my way to the bathroom to get to the mirror, I wiped my palm across my face to find the cut and stop the flow. I pulled my hand away to see not blood but water. I tasted it and recognized it for tears. I hadn't cut myself. I was crying.

When Hiko got home, I waited in the living room, facing where the television used to be. She called and I answered, and she felt her way toward me.

She said, "My God, how did this happen?"

She'd heard about the jump from Karen. I wanted to call it "the accident" but couldn't. Accidents are things that aren't meant to happen. There was no avoiding this.

"I'm fine," I said. "By the way, we were robbed. They took my TV."

"Oh God."

I told her it was fine. That everything would be all right. I didn't need a TV, I said. I never wanted another. Not while films of Mal were being shown. I said all this while she held me. Inside I thought, *Not while sex tapes of me are being shown.*

MAL'S FUNERAL WAS small and quiet and Karen cried through the entire ceremony. Deep into fall, the sky hung low and the leaves were gone. The cemetery was surrounded by a gray haze of barren trees that refused to move despite the wind. Afterward, as everyone else began to leave, I stayed beside the grave, safer and calmer there than anywhere I'd been in weeks.

Karen was comforted by her mother and Hiko. She pointed at me and then separated from them. I thought she would go to the car, to leave the cemetery, but she came directly to me. "We need to talk."

"Of course."

"Not here. Tomorrow, come to my place. Bring anything of Mal's that you still have."

"I don't know if I—"

"Just look around. You might have something. It's mine now and I want it. Even if you don't have anything, come to my place tomorrow at two." She walked away without looking back.

This left me rattled. I'd always thought that Karen didn't like me. Much the same way that I thought Hiko didn't like Mal. We formed an odd circle, Mal to Karen to me to Hiko. Neither woman trusting the other's man, neither man quite trusting the other. What had kept us together, what kept us from pushing the others away, was an emotional gravity that keeps people in orbit despite so many reasons for them to tear free and float by themselves. Now, without Mal, Karen would probably break free, and there was nothing to keep her from ripping into me on her way out.

There had been something in her voice, I thought. Something present in its lack, something that told me she'd decided enough was enough.

Later that afternoon I made up another lame excuse to Hiko. I said I was going to do some research at the library or a bookstore, looking for information on my "condition." I went to Emilia's.

At first she didn't want me to come up to her place. I ignored the fact that she had ended our nonrelationship, I ignored the fact that I had convinced myself that the ending hadn't happened. I stood outside her building and pushed on the buzzer over and over until she finally let me up.

She met me at her door, no smile on her face and no clothes on her body. There were packed boxes throughout the apartment, small spaces barely left for a chair here or a pile of magazines there. She took my hand and with a sad resignation took me to her bedroom and lay down with me.

Afterward, feeling the sweat roll off my sides and mix with the pale bloody spots on her sheets, I realized that my patterns and habits revolved more and more around Emilia, with fewer of my moments spent around Hiko. Hiko demanded more somehow, and I was ready to move away from that. I drifted between two islands, it seemed. One was more dangerous but was closer, and so I tried to reach land. Even though Emilia and I didn't really talk, I thought there must be some sort of security there.

Emilia got up and left the room.

Still lying on her bed, I said, "So, I've been thinking about California." I hadn't been, but I grew more scared by the moment that an ending, a bad one, approached. Mal gone, Karen demanding something from me. I drifted.

Emilia sat in the bathroom, gasping as she dripped hydrogen peroxide into the small cuts and bite marks I'd just left on her body. I'd once offered to clean them for her, but she'd laughed and said that I only needed to worry about what I did *to* her, not what I could do *for* her. I didn't understand the difference.

I said, "I've been thinking about it a lot, and I was thinking, I could go with you."

She didn't respond, so I rolled off the bed and went to the bathroom door and repeated the offer.

"I heard you," she said. She didn't look at me. She sat on the closed toilet lid, dabbing a cotton ball over a cut on her thigh. When had I done that? I couldn't recall. The white panties she wore had a drop of blood on them. I wondered at how many articles of clothing might have been ruined during our time together.

"So," I said, "what do you think?"

"Why are you asking?" She concentrated on her wounds. Mine could wait.

"I guess I'm trying to figure out where I might be in the next few years."

She smirked and her eyes flashed at me. She stood and tossed some bloody cotton balls into the garbage. "Jesus. You actually, what, see us settling down somewhere? With some little house and a yard and a fence?"

My stupidity rushed over me and I felt suddenly sweaty. I walked back to the bedroom. "Where are my clothes?"

The medicine cabinet snapped open and shut as she pulled out a box of bandages. She followed me into the bedroom and threw them on the bed. "We don't even live together, for God's sake."

I pulled my jeans on. Before pulling on my shirt I realized that I hadn't cleaned my newest wounds from the afternoon spent bloodying her bed. They still wept blood and should have been cleaned and bandaged. Instead I pulled the shirt on. The blood would show through it, probably ruin it, but I had to get out of her apartment.

Emilia stood in the doorway, watching me. She was skinnier than I remembered, thinner by a hand's width.

She said, "I mean, what were you hoping for?"

I grabbed my shoes and pulled one on. "I don't know." I really didn't. "I don't think I hope for anything."

"Well, you must. You asked the question, and you're upset at my answer." She disappeared into the bathroom again.

I tried to imagine she was right, but I couldn't decide what I hoped for, if anything. Somewhere beneath my annoyance at her answers, my fears about Hiko discovering my relationship, my distrust of Mal and Michael and others who cheered on my performances or claimed rights due to friendship, somewhere under all of that there must have been some sort of hope or expectation. There had to be. Mal would have known what he wanted. He would have demanded and gotten an answer from her.

I tried to find a path back to her front door, but boxes blocked me in. I looked over the walls of stacked cartons, wondered what they were filled with and how I'd gotten past them. Emilia stood in the hallway and watched me try to go.

"I know you're upset about your friend dying, but that doesn't mean that you and I have something more than whatever this was."

I shut the door behind me. I was left with little consolation other than the fact that she would take some small part of me with her to California. It would be the little black flecks of blood sprinkled over her sheets and clothes, unless she managed to do some laundry before leaving.

The next day I went to the tiny apartment Karen and Mal had shared and which Karen now haunted alone. New pictures peppered the walls. Karen let me walk around for a moment, as if in a museum. I examined each picture and, sadly, found most of them were of Karen and Mal. He looked happier in the pictures than I remembered him to be in person. Many were taken at parties or bars, with dark crowds behind and lighting that caught the sweat and exhaustion on him and Karen. There was one black-and-white photo taken in a park.

They were walking away from the camera and looking at each other, smiling, clearly happy in a way only they knew. The picture caught and held me. I fingered the scar on the back of my hand where I'd stapled my most recent cut shut.

Karen circled through the room, unsure what to do with me there. "So you didn't find anything?"

"No, sorry. I had some stuff, but Mal took it."

"The jump equipment, right? I had a feeling he was going to do something incredibly stupid, so I made him throw it out. I believed him when he said he had. But you had it, right? You held it for him."

Karen stood in her kitchen and tried to avoid looking at me as she put dishes away.

I said, "I looked around, but I didn't have anything else." She waved my comment away.

"I really don't care about that anymore. Until last night I wanted to get a hold of everything of his that I could. I didn't know what I wanted it for, but I knew I wanted it. Then I suddenly had an idea. I literally thought, *I'll take all the bastard's stuff and I'll burn it*. Can you believe that? For a second I didn't remember how he died. I was just so mad I thought, *Burn it*."

Her eyes filled with tears and she put a chipped blue dish on the counter and walked away. I'd never been in the apartment during the day. Brilliant sunlight poured through the windows. Outside, kids filled a basketball court with pleasant screams. I longed to be out there.

I wanted to be near laughter, anywhere I could find it, even on a basketball court filled with strangers.

I said, "Why don't we go outside for a quick walk?"

"No. I just wanted to talk to you for a moment, then you can go." She sat down on the threadbare sofa and searched around a second, then found a pile of papers and flipped through them. "I just wanted to let you know that there's some stuff of you online."

I didn't know how this related to Mal. "Some of the old videos? Me with a lion?"

"No, new stuff. You having sex."

She pulled a page from the pile and held it out for me. At first I couldn't figure out what angle to view the grainy image from. Finally, I realized it was a shot of a window and through the window were two people on a bed.

Karen leaned back, the pile of papers on her lap. "I was doing research on you and found this. About two days ago."

"This doesn't look like me."

"Not that shot, but that's only the still that I printed out. The film is pretty clear, actually. Some guy sneaking around on fire escapes and he gets that. He recognized you and now it's out there for the world. It's you and some model. She's wearing tiger gloves."

The paper got terribly heavy. Had there really been someone on the fire escape and wouldn't I have noticed? As I remembered everything that Emilia had done, I realized that I probably wouldn't have noticed at all.

Karen stood up and took the paper back. "You two do some pretty twisted shit. You I understand, you can't feel it. But her?"

She walked to the kitchen. When she came back she had a glass of water. She sipped at it cautiously while I tried to get my brain to work.

She put the glass down. "I wanted to tell you so that you can do the right thing and break up with Hiko."

I blinked hard a few times, to regain focus I probably never had. "How is any of this your business?" I crinkled the paper but knew I couldn't really destroy the image it had left in my head or the dozens of other images tied to it from my many visits to Emilia.

"She's my friend. As her friend, I will keep her away from people who will do stupid things that might hurt her. You're doing that."

I tried to call her bluff. "I'll tell her."

"No, you won't."

It was final. The way she cut the words off shut my mouth and held it closed, almost as if it had been stapled shut.

She walked back to the kitchen sink and refilled her glass. As she dropped ice cubes into it she glanced over her shoulder and finally looked fully at me. "You've done nothing but stand by and watch as people self-destruct around you. Now I'm going to make sure that you don't drag my friend down like Mal did me."

"This will hurt her."

"You hurt her. You hurt me. You hurt Mal. You could have stopped him. All he wanted was everything you fell into. You just stood there and watched him kill himself for something you don't even want, apparently."

"I didn't do anything to Mal."

"No, and I'm probably not being fair, but I don't care. What I'm going to do is tell Hiko. So get the hell out so I can make a phone call."

I thought I should be angry, but I couldn't bring myself to feel it. Instead I had shame, and lots of it. I felt shorter than Karen, like a child caught doing horrible things and knowing that soon punishment would fall, punishment deserving and terrible. I stumbled for the door and when I turned to look at her, to make one last attempt to stop her, I realized I couldn't. I had done nothing to stop Mal, and maybe that amounted to pushing him. I'd not stopped him and he'd died. So I left the apartment, and as I pulled the door shut I thought that I was making my leap, just as Mal had, only mine was in the faith that Hiko wouldn't believe the news that Karen was going to tell her. I made that leap. And as I did I knew that Mal had known the moment he left the bridge that he was a dead man.

Karen kept her promise. When I got home, I found Hiko crying in the living room. I stood by the door for nearly an hour as she cried, just watching her, waiting for her to talk to me. The only thing she wanted from me was to feel the cuts and bruises Emilia had left on me. She demanded, not requested, this.

"Why do you want that?" I asked. "You don't want that. It's perverse."

"No more perverse than being taped fucking some bitch who stabbed herself with a fork."

I was amazed at how much information Karen had shared. Apparently nothing had been left out. I said, "How was I to know I was being taped?"

"You've been complaining about being taped doing everything else. Now you've been taped screwing some-one. What the hell did you think? Her windows were open, for God's sake."

She sat rigid, her back straight. Her body quivered. She said, "I always thought I would lose you when you got your memory back. I never thought it would be to some bitch with claws you met at a photo shoot."

I didn't say anything for a minute. "For a blind woman you sure know a lot about the tape."

She threw her glasses at my voice. She stood there with her eyes wide. I felt like I'd just punched her in the stomach. Her face screwed up as her anger tortured her.

I apologized and took off my shirt and pants. "Come over here," I said.

I took her hands and guided them to my sides. Her fingers played over my cuts, the raised welts of the scratches. On her face played the pain from them that I hadn't felt.

After running her hands down my thighs and across my back, she stood before me and I reached out to touch her face. She pushed my hand away.

She said, "I never want to see you again." She said it without any edge or tone. It was the most perfect thing anyone had ever said to me. I remained surrounded by strangers who couldn't get enough of me, and intimate friends who couldn't stand the sight of me.

"Get out."

I'd already thrown most of my belongings out the window, so there was little packing. I left with just a bag of clothes. I moved back to the hotel.

About two weeks after I left I tried calling. She wouldn't answer.

eleven

I'D BEEN AT the hotel for a month, spending my time the only way I knew how, and I had the dog-eared magazines and newspapers to prove it. Coverage of Mal's death had started in the tabloids and drifted into the currents that ran past mainstream newsmagazines. *Time*, *Newsweek*, even the *New York Times* picked up on the story, broadened its scope, tethered it to me, and then made me a touchstone of the independent video underground, the reality-video revolution and its impact on commercial entertainment. I refused all calls for comment. I was shown in frame-grab photos in the articles and distrusted even Michael when he told me that he could vouch for a certain reporter and that an upcoming article would be about Mal himself and not simply an opportunity to reference me and my accidental exploits.

Michael contacted me with his plan when copycat videos started to appear.

One late afternoon, rain pouring outside, I was watching CNN, sound muted, closed captioning on, when a video came on of someone who might have been me but for thirty extra pounds around the middle and a dragon tattoo across his left biceps. His face grimaced and his lips turned pale as a three-foot steel wire pierced above and below the line of his mouth, what I imagine was an offensive orifice, sewn shut. CNN's caption below this video laid his stupidity at my feet with the simple exclamation: *Numb-a-like.*

My phone rang and the debate between raising the television volume or answering the phone lasted only to the end of "Hello." It was Michael. He would help me get through my troubles and make money at the same time.

"You go to California." He told me about recent interest in getting me into some films, possible guest spots on television. He promised exactly the opposite of what he'd done earlier. I could be sold now.

"What sort of films would they be?"

"Stuff you could relate to."

I figured that meant they would be about me.

"You haven't been to LA. You should go. Get out of New York and get some sun. It's depressing enough here and you've had too much bad shit happen recently."

I sat on the hotel bed, phone pressed to my ear. Above the dresser hung a mirror and I could see the mess of sheets around me, the wet towels, the scars on my sides and shoulders, the dark circles under my eyes. I looked like Mal had when I'd run into him at the gallery. Shallow and empty. Karen's story about Mal's car wreck crashed into my head. California was probably the last place I should go, but I suddenly felt as if I'd already been there and would be revisiting what Mal and I had done before, as if Mal had promised me something that only California could give.

I said, "Why the sudden interest in me? When I suggested California months ago you said there wasn't any project for me."

I could hear a pencil tapping on Michael's desk as he tried to think of what to say.

"It's because of Mal's death, right?"

The pencil stopped.

"Or it's that sex tape. Whatever. Okay, I'll go."

TWO WEEKS LATER I took a cab to the airport. On the cab's backseat lay a rumpled *Star* magazine. Whoever had left it behind had used it well. It was dog-eared and torn. I saw it from upside down and the woman on the cover looked like Hiko. She had dark hair but no glasses. I turned it right side up to see Emilia. I realized how dirty the pages were.

I opened it slowly. The first page of the article about her was a large photo of her in a red tank top and black pants. She held her stomach and laughed at the camera. Her teeth were bigger than I remembered. I skimmed over the article. She was in "another" movie and I tried to remember when she'd been in a first. She "enjoyed modeling" but didn't have a lot of time for it. Los Angeles was "super fast" and she lived near Hollywood but "missed her New York City place."

Then I saw my name. "She still sees the enigmatic performer whose pain resistance was demonstrated when a film of them engaged in a rough intimacy wound up on the Web."

It went on to say that I lived near her and we flew in and out of LA together. The article ended with a photo of Emilia and a man, his arm around her waist, both in baseball caps, walking away from the camera. "They make time for each other, whenever possible," it said.

I immediately called Michael.

"Have you seen the *Star* article with Emilia?"

"You aren't hung up on her, are you?"

"No. Did you read the article?"

"Why?"

"It says she and I are still together. It has pictures that aren't me saying it is."

"Let me call you back."

The cab was worming its way along Lexington when he called back. "Okay, so now I've seen it. Probably they had an old photo."

"What?"

"They usually put these pieces together way in advance. Old interviews, old photos. Don't worry about it."

"It's not me in the picture," I yelled, and the cabbie shot me a glance. He had his own cell phone to his ear and I was a distraction.

"No shit?" Michael said. I could hear him flipping through a magazine. We were both looking at the same images. "Really, you're serious? Looks just like you."

Almost immediately all of Mal's friends had turned to the press and sold their stories, even those who didn't have one. On the plane to LA I was surrounded by people reading another of the gossip rags. On the cover was an old photo of Mal with an inset of him being lifted from the river. *Life and death on the edge,* it said.

A female flight attendant recognized me and flirted with me throughout the flight. She made sure to get a copy of the magazine for me, offered it as if I had any interest in reading about the life and death of the friend I'd watched die, and when I took it and thanked her and put it into my jacket pocket I wondered what was wrong with me that I couldn't just tell her to leave me alone, to take the magazine away, to forget that she had seen me and that we had ever talked. We landed and I gave an autograph and phone number to her. It wasn't my number. I gave her Mal's old number.

I arrived at my hotel in LA and outside the window was an incredibly different view from the one from my hotel in New York City. A sprawl of low buildings led toward mountains in the distance. Other than that, the room was identical to my hotel room in New York. Not the same color, and larger, laid out differently and full of natural light. Still, it was identical. Mail stacked on a bedside table, forwarded by Michael from New York. I assumed Michael had arranged things, considering the anal-retentive touches. The phone messages were stacked in chronological order and the mail sorted into four piles: junk, bills, personal, and miscellaneous. Miscellaneous was anything bigger than a letter. There were magazines, a set of glossy photos of more models for me to choose from for an upcoming photo shoot, and scripts in large manila envelopes.

I sat on a sofa that faced the windows. I pulled my jacket off and the magazine slipped to the floor. I bent and picked it up and, despite my disgust at it, opened it and flipped through to the pages about Mal's life. Photos purchased from the hangers-on and spectators mixed with professional images of the places that Mal had lived. The story even worked in his time in California: it referred to his car accident and had an image of the building where he'd stayed. I stopped flipping the pages and focused on the California images and text. I read back and forth through the pages to see if I could gather anything more than what little I knew. I couldn't. I had a photo of the place he'd lived in downtown Los Angeles, a warehouse turned apartment complex, crumbling arch entrance guarded by massive jade plants crawling from ignored planters on either side. I sat with the magazine in my lap until I heard my stomach growl. I looked up, found the sun mostly set, the buildings visible from my window painted red, and the mountains beyond them glowing orange. My last meal had been airplane food more than eighteen hours earlier. What kind of fugue state had I fallen into? I rolled up the magazine, returned it to my jacket pocket, and headed to the door.

At the front desk I asked for directions to nearby restaurants. I was in Santa Monica, and they directed me to the Promenade. I walked the two blocks and found it, a wide street closed to vehicles, with large sculptured shrubs down the center. Fountains splattered nearby. Pedestrians wandered down the middle of the street, illuminated by the chain stores and restaurants on either side, and walking around the street performers formed small nucleic clusters every block or so.

I tried not to watch the performers, as they reminded me of Mal's and my struggles during our trip to New York. If we'd come to Los Angeles instead, we might have been among them even still, performing for quarters and the occasional bill from tourists coming out of Banana Republic. I went straight into a half-empty Tex-Mex joint and ordered a margarita and a burrito. Seated near the front, I watched street jugglers take turns throwing blades in the air. There were three of them, their routine tightly organized. One worked the crowd as the others passed whirling machetes back and forth with precise aim and well rehearsed ad-libs. I hadn't wanted to watch, but by the end of my burrito and third margarita I was transfixed by the blades and the banter. I paid my check and gave the waiter an extra ten to call a cab for me. I then walked past the performers and dropped a couple of bills into their coffee can. The one working the crowd stopped in the middle of his spiel and looked at me. He raised a hand, as if to stop the others mid-act, as if to pull the blades from the air and draw his friends' attention to me instead of the dangerous routine they'd perfected. Before he could say anything I gave him another bill and said, "Do us all a favor and pretend you don't know who I am."

His hand fell, as did his grin. He nodded and I waved goodnight as I headed to the corner to wait for my cab. I heard but didn't see the act resume behind me.

When the cab arrived I shoved the magazine toward the driver and showed him the picture of the complex Mal had been in.

"All I know is it's in downtown Los Angeles." The elderly driver nodded and pressed the gas.

I spent seventy dollars on that cab. We drove for hours, up and down streets, most as terrible and vacant as the one before, and I lost the boost of my margaritas and slept for a time. For never having met the driver before, I trusted him deeply, and true to my trust, he woke me when he found the building.

"Hey, here it is."

I pulled myself up from the seat and looked out a window.

"Other side."

I turned and saw it was there, and it looked worse

than the picture had promised. The only thing healthy about it were the jade plants, which had turned to thriving bushes that stretched out and up as if intuiting there was a higher purpose they hadn't yet come to understand. I paid the cabbie and watched him make a quick U-turn to drive back the way he'd come. Only when he turned the corner did I think that I might need him to get back to the hotel.

The street echoed silence. Only a single car rolled toward me, and with the parking lot across the street and warehouses and high-rises nearby I was reminded of a vacant Manhattan.

I approached the arched entrance and stepped quickly out of concern for the cracks that ran across it. On the other side, seated on a bench in a wide entryway and drunk from a shared bottle wrapped in brown paper, conspired three men. Surprised to find them there, I stopped. Surprised to see me stop, they stared, not so much with hostility as with professional concern, professional in this case being drinking and possibly other mind-altering practices and whatever uninhibited viciousness those might accompany.

Just tired enough not to care what they might do to me, I walked up and said, "I'm looking for a guy. A street performer. Lived with someone here." I held up the magazine as if it proved intent or identification, as if I was legitimate because someone in a magazine had once possibly lived in their building.

The tallest also had the worst skin, mottled and acne-scarred, and above his ravaged cheeks sat two pale eyes that looked me up and down. "You mean the guy who killed himself in New York?"

"Yes."

"You a reporter?"

"No. A friend. I want to see where he lived while he was here."

"Friend? Lots of his 'friends' been coming by. They smell a lot like reporters."

"Not me. I smell like a friend."

The two smaller drinkers laughed at this and the taller stepped toward me. We stood in a circle of light from a too-dim lamp. He looked down on me and his eyes, not quite blue, squinted in what amounted to an ocular smile. "I'm sorry for your loss."

I nodded. "Thank you."

"Your friend lived with Bernie up in B-6. Tell him Chump sent you up. He'll talk to you."

"Thanks, Chump."

The tallest shook his head and thumbed toward the shortest of the three. "No, this one's Chump. I'm just the muscle." They all laughed and I tried to as well. As I walked away he called after me again. "You know, you got a sick act."

I counted a few empty thought balloons in my head. "I know."

I walked along an uncertain path that suffered from

sporadic illumination, weaved back and forth between weeds growing from deep cracks, wandered often over stretches with no cement or wood flooring at all, dirt and sand grinding beneath me in the dark. At last I turned a corner and saw some stairs. I climbed them, despite not being certain of where they went other than up, and when I reached the top I found myself looking at a door that had the gold lettering *B-6* glued to it. I knocked and waited for Bernie to answer.

When Bernie finally opened the door I was surprised it hadn't taken longer. His hair and beard, one knottier than the other and sprinkled with bits of paper and cracker, all seemed to be growing leftward with such insistence that I thought not of someone having slept for too long on one side but of a plant left near a window to grow toward sunlight. Behind him radiated his apartment, illuminated by what might have been a thousand lamps of various designs, on the floor, tables, chairs, some on their sides, all burning bright, no lampshades, their heat rolling out from the open door and radiating across my face and head as it spilled up into the cooler evening air. He staggered and squinted. He smelled of moss and water. I wondered if he might not wither if taken into the dry darkness outside, if I might have caused him harm just by letting in a chill.

He looked me in the eye best he could. "Who is it?"

"Chump sent me up. I was a friend of Mal's."

His waver stopped for a moment. "Not a reporter?"

"Not according to Chump."

"Chump's got good instincts. Come on in."

I followed him in and stood at the door a moment as my eyes adjusted. Bernie stagger-stepped heavy, awkward stomps, yet missed every lamp and bulb, broke nothing, as he moved across the loft's large room to a curtain and disappeared behind it. If some of the lights between me and the curtain had been extinguished, I might have enjoyed a shadow-puppet show, as there were at least a dozen burning bulbs on the other side. The heat of the room was unbearable. Extension cords ran the floor like a web, lamps plugged into one that connected to another that was already connected to three or more cords and lamps. The cords crossed one another, three or four thick, gathered in clumps, leading back to a single source cord, the primary root, a thumb-thick industrial-orange extension that curled on the floor for seven or eight feet and then shot straight up to the ceiling, to a hole chiseled into the thick plaster and on through wooden slats to a main junction box deep in the ceiling. Modern wiring spiraled out of the junction, siphoning off the juice meant for some other part of the building and delivering it to the free-hanging outlet that the thick orange cord plugged into. Bernie's network fed off stolen voltage that fell from the ceiling. The room was a swirl of electric current and light, and once I grew accustomed to the heat, something that had seemed impossible upon my entrance, I began to sense a jingling along the hairs of my back, the electricity in the air, warping and weaving around me. The tingle ran straight up my spine and danced across the back of my skull.

Bernie came back around the curtain a little more awake, a little less bleary. He stood before me, hands in pockets, sniffing, licking his lips. I remembered then that Karen had called him a drug dealer and wondered if it had been exaggeration or accurate. I saw nothing in the room that looked illegal. In fact, other than the lamps all I saw was a curtain, part of a mattress on the floor behind it, and a box spilling pornographic magazines.

Bernie waited for me to explain my visit, and the fact that I didn't know what I wanted or expected from him stood between us. I pointed at the lamps nearest to us, hoping to find my way by starting with small talk.

"Could we turn off a few of these lights?"

"No."

"Uh . . ."

"Because fuck my landlord, that's why."

"I didn't—"

"Your friend was an okay guy, but we were roommates, not buds. He and I didn't really get along, okay? Fact is, he ruined my car. So if there's something you need other than his things, you can ask or not, I don't care, but do it now 'cause I'm too tired to fuck around."

"His things?"

Bernie pointed at the box of porn. "Might be a few more things at the bottom of the closet, but I can't tell anymore. He was only here a short time and that was months ago."

"Right. Can I?" Already heading for the box, standing it up, riffling.

"Help yourself." Bernie sat on his mattress and munched saltines from an open box. He watched me with the same interest one watches rain, to see what it touches and whether the wetness amounts to anything.

Beneath a thin layer of skin magazines I found a stack of books and article clippings. The books tended toward literature and self-help. Dickens and Powers. *The Stranger* and *Wishcraft*. Beneath these were clippings from newspapers and printouts from a computer I didn't see in the box. I looked toward Bernie, still watching from his bed, fresh crumbs salting the hair of his beard, and wondered if he might have sold some computer Mal had owned. The clips and articles all dealt with freakish stories, bizarre accidents, or ill-advised stunts. The oldest of them, from only a few days after my final Redbach show, placing Mal already in LA much earlier than I could have imagined, was of a woman who, through no fault of her own, wound up with her hand stuck inside a vending machine. At work late, she'd struggled with an insubordinate soda dispenser and lost. It had been a Friday, after hours, so she was forced to wait through the weekend and most of Monday morning until a coworker finally came to get a diet soda and found her, unconscious, on her knees, pressed against the side of the machine, in a pool of her own fluids. Stories and printouts from the same period revolved around similar random accidents and poor plans. Circus-performer accidents were popular with him. As I flipped through the pages I saw the focus narrow over time to self-inflicted acts, public stunts that drew wild attention. Magicians who dared to put on uneventful performances in public—standing in ice, lying in water, suspending themselves above the ground for days. Climbers who scaled office buildings, sculptures, bridges, only to be arrested. Actors and musicians who insisted on public acts of personal distaste. Again the articles refocused and became about certain of these performers, and then re-refocused, toward one in particular. Me.

The first references to me were online pieces about "freakish" acts that had taken place in a circus somewhere, or a bar, or on a street. The printed images were grainy, poor copies of video frames. It was a homemade version of the research that had trailed out of Michael's office, pages fluttering and worn, yellowed with age and poor care in Bernie's closet. Mal, it was obvious, had been on the same trail as Michael's investigators, even having references to some events that they hadn't found, such as the cook who, at the height of the dinner rush, neglected to notice that he had severed and served a finger in a Caesar salad, or the construction worker who had been riveted without much complaint to a high-rise in Dallas. The pages lacked any of the notes or insane speculation of Michael's, but they centered on the same subject. I saw myself in each one. And when I found a DVD with no label near the bottom of the pile of papers I wondered if I was in this too, in exactly the same way. Was I on the disk by not being visible, by being not the one on screen but hunted for nonetheless?

I held the disk up and waved it at Bernie. The light from dozens of bulbs cast circular reflections on the walls around us, as if we were trapped inside a diamond. Bernie blinked out of his meditation on me and raised an eyebrow, something of an effort given the totality of hair across his face.

"Do you have a way to play a DVD?"

"Uh-huh."

A slow minute later he finally stood, knocking half-crackers from his beard as he did so, then fumbled through a closet, its door hidden behind a hanging blanket. When he returned with an old laptop we exchanged a silent accusation and denial that it had once been Mal's, and I turned it on and loaded the disk. It played without prompting, having dreamt of the moment for so long at the box's bottom.

There was a burst of humming and some scratchy feedback. I played with the volume and the bass and treble. The hum never stopped. Occasionally a pop or crackle rose up. Nothing else. I stopped the playback and started it again. It played the same crackle and hiss as before.

The camera technique was nonexistent, wavy and shaky and panning fast enough to make you think of a tennis match. Aside from the setting—the bottles on the cart, the medical apparatus, the stethoscopes and white masks, it looked like any hospital—the film had all the unmistakable signs of a home movie, either a reel-film camera or a very early video with no sound, or one in which the sound had been lost or damaged somehow.

It began with a long shot of a man's back. When he turned toward the camera, he was all mustache. He said something to the camera and then stepped aside and behind him rested a baby on a table. Instinctively I wondered if the baby was me.

The baby sat awkwardly and drooled on itself and made fists that it shook in the air and then stuffed, whole, into its mouth. It wore a little blue jumper with a teddy bear on the front. Clouds were painted on the wall behind the baby.

The camera spun, blurring the room, to a doorway. In it stood a man with the unmistakable air of a doctor. White coat, hand in pocket, stethoscope, heavy sideburns and thick, wavy hair. The mustached man approached the doctor and said something that could have been "How do you do?" or "How are you?" The doctor rubbed the side of his face, blocking his mouth, but whatever he said made the mustached man laugh.

The doctor and the mustached man both moved toward the camera, their smiles nervous, and the mustached man reached out to it. There was a white flash as the image cut to a woman standing next to the baby on the table. The doctor stood next to her. Apparently the mustached man now held the camera. The woman, with long, straight brown hair, fidgeted nervously with her blouse as the doctor examined the baby. The baby kicked and put the stethoscope in its mouth, looked at the ceiling, the woman, the doctor, sometimes at nothing. The doctor weighed the baby, measured the baby, held the baby as a nurse came into the picture and took the child.

Another cut and the image was closer and the doctor held a syringe with a needle and the nurse held the baby. In the background, over the doctor's shoulder, stood the woman, holding her face in her hands. The doctor explained something to her, either ready to give a shot or take blood. The woman looked nervous.

The doctor had the needle, and the baby was in the nurse's arms, and she talked to the baby and the baby looked at the nurse and was excited and kicked as the doctor stepped forward, still looking at the woman, and the needle stuck straight through the baby's fat leg.

The doctor let go, and the syringe hung from the baby, pierced straight through, the shiny point visible through one side, the syringe on the other. The woman screamed and the doctor quickly grabbed the baby's arm and the camera fell down. After another cut the image was of the baby, held by the nurse, and it was unclear who was behind the camera, but the doctor pulled the syringe from the leg, plump and pink, and the baby had a fist in its mouth and didn't react with pain or even interest, and looked at the camera and drooled as the fist left its mouth.

The film jumped then to another room and another doctor. This time the camera seemed to be on a stand—the shot was very level and the image sharper. The baby sat on an examining table and two men in white coats stood nearby. The baby was naked and fat and happy. It held a teething ring in one hand and shook it happily.

The camera moved to the left, toward a tray filled with pins and syringes. One of the men poured alcohol over the utensils, put on rubber gloves, and began to pull pins from the tray. The other man took hold of the baby's arm and held it steady.

I turned off the DVD.

I watched my hands as they floated over the computer keyboard. The scars glowed in its blue light, even some that had faded, some I'd forgotten. An image, stuck on the doctor's hands holding the baby's arm still, floated in my eyes after I shut down the video player. I became aware of breathing behind me and looked over my shoulder into Bernie's twisted mane.

He blew a silent whistle. "It would suck to be that baby."

"Yeah."

"Wonder what Mal was doing with that."

I thought I knew. Mal had protected me once again. He could have sold that video, or sent it to Michael or me or any of the news agencies, when I made my rounds on the talk shows. Instead, he'd sat on it, hidden it away in a box under useless research and pornography. He'd left it behind when he returned to New York. It was past; it hadn't mattered, to him at least. And when I realized that, it began to matter less to me. It might be me, it might not. Mal had died with it in his head. The images wouldn't leave me either, I knew, but he'd kept them where they belonged. What was I to do with them? Nothing could be done. Whomever that was, me or someone else, grown or gone on to other currents, it didn't matter. I looked past Bernie and saw the knots and loops of electrical cords, the repeated patterns, unintentional, but one cord followed close, so close as to almost get it right, the path of one below it, though missing, just by a hair, the same route. This was me and Mal. He'd held on to the video, left it behind, knowing that all it might do was lead me to a place that had no resolution, that with it in my hands I could do nothing about it but watch and watch again. He'd died without sharing it, a form of protection.

Which was absurd. I knew it. Mal had reasons for doing what he'd done, but to see him as protecting me at every step was both unfair to him and ridiculous. Mal's research was as much about his need to see the birth of fame as it was about looking for me. He'd followed that path of self-creation to a fiery end. This film showed me no proof, nor did I have proof Mal had wanted to protect me. That didn't matter. I could behave as if I did. I could behave however I liked. If I needed to find solace and protection in the video, if I needed to find permission to stop hauling up questions about my past, like luggage I neither owned nor cared for, then I would give those to myself. I could be as free of these questions as I wanted, and behave as if I either knew myself or didn't. Either way, I thought, I would find out.

Bernie had retreated to his bed and crackers. I stood and looked around the room. It suddenly felt rather cozy, and through the windows I could see the brightening sky. Dawn approached. Buildings outside glowed blue, subtly showing some inner light at the edges and even glimmering in their darkened windows, as if sleepers there released energy to the building and the building released it to the morning, somehow leaking what was normally held inside.

I said, "Would you have a car I could borrow?"

Bernie shook his head. "Told you. Mal ruined it. Haven't replaced it yet."

"Where did he do that?"

"Northbound I-5, I think. Near the Indiana exit."

I stood at the center of the room, looking from the cords to the computer to Bernie, realizing I wanted none of Mal's things, disk included, and held a hand up to Bernie. "Thanks for your help."

He nodded, his mouthful of crackers ending any reply. I stepped over the cords and what I saw now were tiny bits of broken bulbs, a shimmering dust that sprinkled the floor. I crossed to the door and left. The light in the hall was nonexistent and I groped my way down the stairs and back to the arch. Chump and his muscle had gone.

Outside, the light fell short of Bernie's room. I watched a few cars pass as my eyes adjusted and then realized that a cab sat parked in front of the building. I stooped to ask for a ride and found the driver was the same gray-haired man who'd brought me.

"What are you doing here?"

He held up a brown bag. "You forgot your leftovers. Thought I might find you."

"Those aren't my leftovers."

We both looked at the bag as if it might tell us who had left it. Finally he said, "Well, shit. Just trying to do the decent thing here."

Most decency is inexplicable, I realized. Mal had had his. This driver had his. I aspired to that level of confusion, of doing the wrong thing for the right reasons.

"Can you give me a ride?"

"Sure. Get in."

The driver probably should have argued with me when I told him to slow down and then stop in the breakdown lane of I-5. He puzzled me by not only doing so but doing so with a smile. The car swayed as an eighteen-wheeler passed within a foot of us, sucking the air away from the side of the car and forcing us to lean toward it for an instant before buffeting away. When the car fully settled I said, "I'll be right back, but you don't have to stay if you don't feel safe." He shrugged and I climbed out.

Two hundred feet behind the car, chiseled into the cement wall that ran alongside the highway, black grooves and tire marks ran up the dirty white barricade. Something had slammed into it and then burned. Glass littered the ground, red and clear plastic shards sprinkled in, as well as long strips of aluminum. I ran my hands over the wall. I knelt and looked into the gouges. I felt the tire marks. Trucks hammered me with horns and rushing air. To my left shook the cab, stoic as a tombstone. I returned to it and climbed in.

The driver was kind enough to not look at me for too long in the mirror. "You find what you need?"

"I don't know."

He swallowed. "You want some of this leftover food? It's Chinese."

"No thanks. How about finding me a pay phone?"

He didn't start the car. Instead, he handed me his cell phone.

I dialed Michael.

After he woke himself up enough to realize it was me he said, "Where the fuck have you been?"

"Seeing the city."

"You absolutely blew off our meeting with the studio

last night. They weren't pleased, so I lied and said you were sick. When we see them today, make sure to look sick."

I didn't say anything. I watched an airplane fly overhead and thought about the airport.

Michael said, "The project you signed on to, it's moving forward."

"Is this an *about* me or a *with* me?"

"Both."

"How's that possible?"

"Well, as I said, the contract covers all aspects of your story, known or unknown. They've looked into it, and your story remains unknown in a big way. No investigator found a thing about you. That's theirs and ours. So they are running with a reality formula."

"In other words, making things up."

"Yep."

"But it won't be true."

"True? It won't be true or false, it will be 'inspired by,' and you should consider yourself lucky they don't just grab you as the starting point and run away with it. You should be glad they want you in it at all. They could do some sort of special effects to make someone else into you."

"I should be glad they've cast me in my own story, which they are making up?"

"Exactly."

I wondered how to react to this. I thought about how

I might make it interesting to react as if cameras were there, on the side of the road, behind a cabbie munching on someone's leftover Chinese. It seemed appropriate, starting my performance right away.

I said, "What if I can't do this?"

Michael wanted to get off the phone. "Listen, I don't know why you should be upset. I got you money up front, regardless of whether they found facts or made stuff up. And they don't have to use you, but they are. You came out on top."

"I'm on top." I looked out the window. A trio of trucks sped past and the car filled with a roar as the air was sucked away. When the car settled I said, "So, at least they want me for my own movie."

Michael's smile came through the phone. "That's right. And you're not the only one. They're taking advantage of your current publicity." A slight pause as he realized he'd have to steamroll over the fact that my publicity had come as a result of Mal's death. "They're looking for people who know you to be in it. It's like they've taken reality television to an extreme, casting people from your actual life to play your friends in the film."

"People will play themselves?"

"Yes. They're casting some of it, approaching some of the actuals for the rest."

"What about Hiko?"

Michael, stuttering as he sought a lie, gave a professional laugh. "I—I don't know. Think they might be, you know, approaching her."

The driver munched on his chow mein breakfast. Another truck rumbled by and for a minute I couldn't hear Michael over the roar. He swore and asked where I was.

I ignored him. "Who are these people?"

"Come to the dinner tonight and you'll meet them."

"Dinner?"

"The meal after lunch." He paused to laugh at himself. "Steven, the head man, is having a nice-to-meet-ya at his place in the Hills. You, me, a couple of the producers, Steven, a few of the other, um . . . *actors* doesn't seem like the right word."

"Actors like who?"

"Come see."

I hung up and handed the driver his phone. He pocketed it without looking at it. He was my best friend in LA. "Where to?"

I told him my hotel. I needed to sleep. He pulled back into traffic, raising horrified horns from several trucks in the process, and hummed under his breath as he tossed the empty Chinese container onto the passenger seat. I watched the morning light reach out over the roads, touch broad bands of clouds over the ocean. In New York it would be midmorning. Hiko would be up and beginning her day, preparing to work in her studio or finding her way to a gallery or a teaching gig, and possibly stewing over the audacity of movie producers asking for her not due to beauty or talent but because she had the bad luck to have allowed me into her home.

twelve

AS I HAD prayed for on the drive to the hotel, I fell asleep easily and slept most of the day undisturbed. As late-afternoon light fell across the bed through a gap in the curtains I woke, blinked at the orange rays, and wondered for a full minute where I was before the pile of mail on the coffee table reminded me.

I dressed and headed to the lobby. Michael sat in the bar. I waited for him while he finished his drink, then he walked from the bar to me by way of the main desk to check for messages I'm sure he knew were not there. I walked past him and he fell into my wake. We climbed into a cab.

Michael talked for most of the trip, on his phone and to me, sometimes at the same time. Words fell from him like rocks into water, disappeared and forgotten after the initial splash. I watched the sides of the road, the barricades and guard rails. I hunted for scratches, dents, any sign of collision. I counted them on my fingers, like a collector. I didn't know what purpose they served, but even when I realized what I was doing I continued and felt a small glimmer when I saw broken glass at a corner or black rubber skid marks end far too suddenly in an intersection.

We reached the house within thirty minutes and Michael, cell phone off and in his pocket, gazed up at the three-story Spanish villa. "Look at that."

I looked, unsure whether he meant the house or something particular. Lit with spotlights hidden by landscaping, it radiated an artificial quality. Every detail of the architecture stood out, despite the fact that the sun was setting behind it and it should have been backlit, dark and hard to see instead of full and fresh and looking like dawn touched nowhere else. I followed Michael to the front door. Before he could knock, it swung open and a middle-aged man in a white cotton shirt and khakis held his hands out to me and Michael. He was bearded, pale across his face and neck, tanned from elbow to wrist. I guessed he spent his time behind the wheel of a car, stuck in traffic, making deals on a cell phone.

"You're here," he said. Michael held his right hand and I gripped the left, both of us one step lower than our host, penitents to a saint. His smile bordered on beatific. "I'm so excited you made it."

Michael introduced me to Steven. We continued our awkward left-hand-right-hand shake. Steven said, "Feeling better, I hope?" It seemed genuine sympathy for my faked illness, and so I mumbled thanks and looked away, which I'm sure gave the impression that we all knew it was a lie.

He wouldn't release me, somehow even spinning his grip so that I now held his hand as children do their parents', and pulled me into the house across an ornate, tiled floor. Looking down I saw he wore no shoes or socks. Michael walked behind me, trapped in a grin I couldn't understand. From the entryway Steven guided us to an expansive living room bordered by windows along one side. Beyond the windows shimmered a lighted and heated pool. Vapors rose from it in the cool evening air. Its too-blue water rippled from a single swimmer, a woman, as she glided along the perimeter.

In the room, barely furnished except for three low chairs and a twelve-foot table covered with white cloth and food and drink, a dozen people swirled around one another. Conversation stopped for a breath when we entered, but most everyone seemed accustomed to ignoring the famous and didn't give any sign of recognizing me beyond darted eyes. Artwork adorned the walls. Made from lightbulbs, all on and generating enough heat and light for four rooms this size, the pieces overlit the room, and I looked through the group of people, expecting to see Bernie. One light box had nine bulbs arranged in a square. Another a circle. I didn't see, but wasn't surprised later to hear about, a triangle. I stared at the square, squinting as I wondered how many bulbs I would meet while in LA.

Steven followed my eyes and leaned toward me. "Great, aren't they? I found an artist downtown who's working exclusively in light."

I nodded and tried to pull my hand away. Steven wouldn't let me. He turned and pulled me into a hug, pressed me chest to chest, stomach to stomach, his beard and breath tickling my ear. "Tell me something, and be honest. I can smell lies. Do you do what you do because of drugs? Are you on something?"

"Uh, no." His breath rolled across my neck. "No drugs."

The hug grew tighter for an instant and then he let go. He leaned back and smiled at me, close enough to know that I'd brushed my teeth, and said, "Good to hear it. Good to know your talent is genuine."

Michael clapped me on the back. They treated me as if I'd just won a prize.

Steven said, "Let's go meet the others."

I circled the crowd with Steven and Michael and was introduced to people whose names meant as little to me as they did to Steven. He'd forgotten half of them and searched for names, awkward, eyes to the ceiling, until the mysterious guests took pity and introduced themselves. Some of them were producers. One woman, a casting agent, was the only one to ask if I might be hungry and kindly offered me a small plate of cheese. Three others were actors being considered for the movie. I couldn't look at them. What was there to see other than strangers?

As if reading my thoughts, the casting agent said, "You'll be glad to know that not all of them are strangers."

"Meaning?"

She pointed toward the pool where the swimmer climbed from the water to be wrapped in a towel held for her by one of the male actors. She rubbed the towel against her sides and pulled it over her head as she headed through a door into a small bathhouse. The actor followed.

"Who was that?" I said.

The agent looked at Michael, a small blush on her cheeks. "I thought you were going to tell him."

Michael leaned over my shoulder and whispered in my ear, "It's Emilia. She'll be playing herself in the film."

I felt as if I'd stepped in something slippery. The door of the bathhouse closed and I watched it for a breath, then turned to Michael and wondered aloud if he'd lost his mind. The guests around us looked at one another, obvious in their avoidance of my gaze, and I held nothing against them as they drifted away from me.

Michael, Steven beside him, stood his ground. "She was integral to the story. It's you, but it's not all you."

I nodded. A flash inside my head as I looked back to the bathhouse. "You represent her, don't you?"

Michael waved a hand at me. "I make no apologies for doing cross promotion that helps everyone." He said *cross promotion* as if it held religious meaning in our situation. Now even Steven looked uncomfortable.

"I thought we'd agreed to have all our cards on the table before proceeding." This was aimed at Michael even as he looked at me. I didn't sense any protective urge for me as much as anger at the discomfort of the "talent" being cantankerous. That was me, I realized, the tempestuous star.

Another few minutes and Emilia emerged from the bathhouse, actor in tow, radiant but not at all how she had been in New York. She was calm, her face softer, and her eyes smiled at me when she walked into the room. She had bare feet and wore a simple white dress that glowed in the heavy lighting from the incandescent artwork. I'd seen her on the cover of some men's magazine and she'd had this look. I'd thought it was makeup and a good art director forcing a change to her style. Turns out it was just her.

She walked straight to me, said, "Hi." A broad grin broke through and she reached for my hand. The Emilia I knew in New York had had a sharp, dangerous edge, and if you wore it down, you would discover the threat of a dull razor. How could she have softened so much to reveal this laid-back spirit?

She walked me to a corner framed on either side by bulb fixtures in the shapes of an X and a plus sign. She walked in slow motion, like a film had been taken of the woman in New York and slowed just slightly to make her more fluid. Beneath the dress a softer energy flowed, and when it pressed out subtly it was even more exciting than the jagged high energy she'd barely contained three months earlier. An entirely new image of her opened in my head, one that blended this Emilia with the one I'd known. This Emilia was deeper, more emotionally grounded, and I realized, seeing the tranquility in her face, how haunted and afraid she had always looked in New York. Maybe I looked the same way.

"You look great," she said. "California does good things for you."

I looked at the plus-sign lights and did some hurried calculations. "I've been here for forty hours."

She laughed. "Guess it just works fast."

She seemed a ghost of someone I hadn't known. Behind me the actor lurked, far enough behind me to not be too present, close enough to remind me I was being watched.

I said, "You look nice."

"Thanks. Southern California agrees with me." She ran her hands over her dress, smoothed the unwrinkled fabric. I could see through it, I thought, see some of the pale scars I knew I'd left behind. She said, "You've really made a name for yourself. No more sideshows. Your own movie."

"Yeah, sort of." I was about to ask for her to help me figure out how a fictional story about a guy like me could be "my" story when a man's voice rose from behind me.

It said, "Who wants wine?"

Rather than introduce me to the lurker, Emilia repeated the question to me as if I hadn't heard. "Would you like some wine?"

I looked over my shoulder at the tall, very fit man with dark hair and features sculptors dream of uncovering. I said, "Wine?"

I must have nodded because Emilia answered, "That's two for wine."

The sculpture disappeared for too brief a time and when he came back he carried three glasses of wine in one hand as if the hand had been made for nothing else.

Emilia took a glass and smiled at him. To me she said, "This is Ray."

Ray said something about being glad to finally meet me. I watched as he moved between me and the X light, became nothing more than a shimmering silhouette, a cutout of a perfect man, complete and happy in his own presence, removed from the room by light and dark. He was at home anywhere, and anywhere he stood became home. I smelled his musk in the air, watched his girlfriend in the white dress, tasted his wine. I looked at what he wanted as his life, and at what he had, and they were the same thing. Emilia was part of it.

One or the other, I cannot remember now who, began

to talk about the wonder of the house and the beauty of the artwork. From there the monologue was shared by both as they spoke without a hint of needing me to contribute or even pretending that I mattered in the conversation. They shared details of their lives that they both already knew with, if not me, as I had asked for none of it, then some unseen audience I felt hidden just behind me, watching from rows of seats trapped in the dark corners away from the lights. I longed to look and see someone in the audience at whom I could raise an eyebrow and ask if there was a need to repeat a line or two.

The two of them smiled at each other every two minutes for reasons invisible to me. They grinned at each other while describing how they'd found their home. When I told them where I was staying they shared a knowing look that went unexplained. And there was definitely a giggle when Emilia mentioned they were going out later that evening. I bumped up against secrets they shared and I felt like I was only there to view them, like animals in a cage. Why had I come? Better yet, why had I been invited?

"So," Ray said, "what exactly was it like, going into that lion's cage?" He said this as if interviewing me, as if the unseen audience had just quieted. I looked around. It wouldn't be the first time that Emilia had put me in a position to be unexpectedly filmed.

"It was a little odd, like it was happening in slow motion." I rubbed the leg with the scar.

Ray nodded. His eyes wide, he turned to face me, pivoting on the sofa. His face caught too much light and he looked manic and pale.

"And when your friend died, you must have been—"

"Ray." Emilia threw a cracker at him. "This isn't one of your workshops." She smiled and shook her head at me. "He's in an acting workshop. He tries to get inside others' experiences and Mal's death is—"

"Unique." Ray took a cube of cheese from his plate and threw it into his mouth.

I thought of a stupid joke that Mal had told me: How do you catch a unique rabbit? Unique up on him.

"Losing Mal was one of the worst things to ever happen to me." I watched a piece of cork float around in my wine. It clung to the side of the glass. Grabbed and carried away by the wine, it stuck somewhere else and hung there for a moment before swirling away again. I knew how the cork felt. I swirled the glass, to give it a chance to get away.

"Worse than your affliction?" Ray leaned forward, eyes locked on mine. He should be taking notes, I thought.

"What affliction?" Of course I knew. I wanted to hear him say it. I wanted to hear how he would describe me and what I could do or couldn't do. I wanted to know how Emilia could stand being in the same room with him for more than five minutes, with his incessant need to own everyone else's emotions, to drain them out for his own use, for his research. I was like a dissected frog, legs splayed, and he was wiring me up to a battery, hoping to make me dance.

"Your nerve damage." He said this as if remarking on someone's hair color. "And your amnesia. You know nothing of your past. How does all that compare to—"

"I don't think of it as an affliction. It's how I am."

"Well, it's not, you know"—he glanced at Emilia for support—"normal."

I can't recall anyone else ever referring to me as "afflicted" to my face. Even The It, who hated me, had never made me feel like I wasn't human. He'd called me a freak, but so was he, and a fake one at that, so it had never made me feel like Ray made me feel. This is how I was. I had no other point of reference. How could it make me feel like anything? It was me.

"Normal?" I put down my wineglass and stood. "You mean, normal like you? With a girlfriend who's got a self-destructive streak and enjoys tormenting former lovers? That kind of normal? Why don't you tell me how you feel knowing that she held forks stuck in my back while she screamed beneath me?"

Emilia shouted at me, "Hey, listen, he's only interested in your relationship to Mal, not—"

"Why?" I yelled. I stood in the middle of the room, my fists tight at my sides, my temples throbbing. Other conversations in the room died as my voice rose. "Why the fuck do you care about him?"

Ray and Emilia shared another private look. No smiles

this time, no giggles. Ray's eyes pleaded with Emilia and she turned away and quietly said, "I thought he knew."

"Knew what?" I startled myself with the command in my voice.

Emilia leaned back. She looked thin again. Around her the light fixtures dimmed from some fluctuation in the lines; the air conditioner's hum dipped a half step for a moment or two. Shadows cut her face back to its old self. Voice as iced as she could muster, she said, "Ray is trying to get the role of Mal in the movie."

Vile words fell from my lips and a woman behind me gasped. I stepped away from fingers that had begun to pull at my shirt buttons, looked down and discovered that the assaulting fingers were my own. I realized what they were up to and looked to see what my words might have done to Emilia. She didn't respond, but Ray blushed. I lowered my shirt and turned my back to Ray.

"I want to show you something, Ray. Does she ever talk about these? These scars, the ones near my waist and the middle of my back. Some are her fingernails, some are pins. Or forks. There's a can opener scar near the small of my back. She used to do this to me while we screwed. Does she do this to you? She got so she couldn't or, more likely, wouldn't do it without cutting as foreplay."

They stood silent, silent as the crowd behind me. The bulbs buzzed at the warm air around us, but I felt cool, my shirt, still tucked in, now hanging at my waist. Emilia, reddened by the lights or anger, seethed, unable to look up from the floor in front of her. Ray looked everywhere but at her. Michael called to me. I ignored him.

I pulled my shirt back on. "I wanted to show you that because it's something Mal knew about. He didn't understand it, but he knew about it. He knew that she tried to peel skin off me while we had sex, and he wondered why I broke the heart of an amazing woman just so I could fool around with Emilia. Mal liked this other woman, my girlfriend Hiko, and he didn't get why I did what I did, but he was my friend and he stood by me while I made my mistakes."

I found my glass of wine and gulped it down. I felt the piece of cork catch at the back of my throat and smiled. "I stood by Mal as he made his mistakes too. Then he became afflicted with death, and Emilia left me for California to help some guy Mal would have hated get into the movies. In fact, I think Mal would have kicked you in the nuts just to see how you'd react."

Ray stiffened to his full height. Easily half a foot taller than me, forty pounds heavier, and in incredible shape. One hand was wrapped around his wineglass, the other whitened to a fist. All I could think was how he would have been awful casting for the part of Mal. We stared at each other and my entire body tensed up, just like it had in Caesar's cage.

My yelling was over. My voice hushed, I said, "Ray, I can't feel pain. So who do you think wins this fight? You with your big muscles, or me with my affliction and a supreme need to work off my hatred of you and Emilia?"

Emilia's voice shook as she told Ray to calm down.

I walked away but could hear Ray say to Emilia, "You said that tape was a publicity stunt."

Steven and Michael chased me to the door but I beat them to it and didn't stop when they called me from it. I looked over my shoulder and saw the two of them crowded in the doorway with other faces behind them, like a logjam collected at the exit of the well-lit house. They called, and I think Steven shook a fist in my direction, or he waved goodbye. Either way, I walked to the street and turned the nearest corner, keeping my hand ready to flag down the next car as I gave a quick prayer it would be a cab.

thirteen

AS SOON AS my plane landed I returned to Hiko's brownstone. I took a taxi from the airport, then sat in it until the meter added an extra two hundred dollars to the tab. For the first thirty minutes we sat there the cabbie complained I was wasting his time. He shut up when I handed him a hundred-dollar bill and told him that was just the tip, if only I could sit a bit longer. When I was ready, I handed him another wad of bills and got out of the cab. Then I stood near a fire hydrant for another half hour.

It was past midnight. Hiko wasn't home; her windows were dark. If she'd been home the windows would have been bright, needlessly illuminated. I imagined her moving through the building, turning on all the lights as she went, allowing them to burn all night. I imagined she wanted to spite her blindness.

Neighboring buildings were mostly dark. A random window occasionally cast white light or the blue-gray flashes of a television screen. A car drove by, followed by a long silence and then another car. No one knew why I was waiting outside the building. No one cared.

I climbed the front steps and reached for the extra key she kept hidden under a window box on a sill near the top step. It was gone. I rechecked, hoping that I had missed it. I hadn't.

I spent ten minutes discovering that picking a lock with a credit card is much harder than in the movies. I mangled a card learning this. I had no idea how to do it anyway. Maybe it only works on a certain kind of lock. My sole victory came while pushing at the lock with my card—the door wasn't closed well to begin with and swung open. My luck ended with the outer door. The inner was locked with a deadbolt.

I closed the outer door and sat on the floor, my back against the wall, and watched the inner door, my bag at my side. I tapped my foot against the inner door and listened to the glass pane of its upper half rattle. I hated what I was about to do. I counted to one hundred, perhaps to give Hiko a chance to get home, perhaps out of fear, and then pulled my hammer from my bag. Airport security in Los Angeles had forced me to check it. The address label and airline sticker hung from the handle.

I held the hammer with both hands and waited for the rumble of the bus that came down the street regularly during the night. It had passed twice since I'd been there and was due soon. At last I heard it laboring toward me. I stood, pulled a T-shirt from my bag, and held it over the window with one hand. As the bus passed, the rumble at its loudest, I brought the hammer around. I put as much force as possible into that shot.

Every time I drove a nail into my skin I had the slightest hesitation, a split second's pulling back, as if to spare myself some pain. I always attributed it to natural instinct, an innate survival code that I couldn't erase. I noticed that same hesitation as the hammer swung through my shirt, shattering the glass window. I noticed the slightest of pauses in my hand, as if saving myself from some sort of pain. Even with that hesitation I'd never hit anything so hard. I'd never even used the hammer on anything but nails aimed at my own skin.

I broke into Hiko's home.

The glass shattered and fell in large, irregular shapes to the floor on both sides of the door. For only a second a sharp, sudden attack of noise enveloped me as the hammer punched through and the glass crashed down, but almost as suddenly the noise stopped. I heard the bus cruising down the street, then nothing but my breath. I reached through the open window and twisted the lock. I entered Hiko's home, crushed glass beneath my feet. In the stucco pattern of the wall I found the light switch. I felt seashells under my wrist as I pushed the switch and the light came on. I wondered if I had ever turned the lights on before. I went through the building repeating this improvement. I turned on every light in every room. I turned on the stereo, and very low Nina Simone drained out. Hiko had even replaced the television I'd owned and then destroyed. I turned it on, with the sound off. Across the screen clung a thin protective plastic film. It was clear and didn't affect the image on the set, but I worked at the corner and caught hold of an edge and peeled it away. It felt as though I was removing the Braille pages I'd taped onto my set, even though it was plastic, not paper, and clearly nothing like the pages I'd cut from Hiko's book. With each light and the stereo and the television, I felt something I'd carried a long time fall from me, and I felt the room open up. I could see it, finally. It was nothing like I remembered. It was warmer, friendlier. Sometimes it's what we carry inside us, I realized, that gives a room its ambiance. It's not the room itself. It's us.

I went to the kitchen and opened all the cupboards. My hand ran along the shelves, feeling the Braille labels under the cans of beans, corn, peas, as my brain tried desperately to memorize their arrangement, to make sense of the small bumps of the labels, to make sense of the random qualities that were organized by Hiko. I did this with a desperation I couldn't fathom. All the cans and boxes were neatly spaced, nicely ordered, but there remained a mystery in why rice sat next to the canned goods, and cereal with the flour and pasta. How could I make sense without Hiko there to guide me through it? She lived through preparation; my hotel life was death by clean towels. I wanted to understand her life so I could help replicate it in myself, copy it, can by can, box by box. I wanted to help prepare something, build something.

I climbed the stairs. The lights in her gallery space came on slowly, and mainly illuminated only the pieces, not the room as a whole. Her personal collection of casts and portraits in stark white glowed under the spotlight halogen bulbs. The heat from each radiated at specific intervals and I realized that was how she knew her place in the room. She counted the gaps between the warmth of the bulbs and the cool spaces in between. I walked past the first ones near the doorway, anxious to get to my own, to find the private face that Hiko had found in me and which terrified me with its infinitely fine spider-webbing of cracks over the surface. I'd been horrified by its accuracy. Now I craved it.

The spot where my portrait had been held something else. Instead of the plain white sculpture I found the horrible, bloody scab portrait, the one that included bits of glass and shards of metal. Hiko had replaced the one that promised what I hoped I could be with what I feared I was. This was the gallery where she kept those works just for her, and I no longer resided there in the way I could have. The harsh, angry image did. Clearly, I'd shattered the other image of myself by my selfish actions, and she'd likely shattered the sculpture because of it.

I left the gallery. In her bedroom I turned on the bedside light. The window ahead reflected me like a mirror. I did not know the person who looked back at me. What faced me exuded disappointment. I saw someone selfish and stupid and hurtful, someone wallowing in ignorant innocence. I saw a man who let a friend die. I saw a man who exchanged trust for lust. I had nothing to show for anything: time, people, places. Nothing I'd done mattered to me or anyone else, and I'd missed so many opportunities for something more. The window reflected the repercussions of that. A worn-out, scarred, and scared man. I didn't know if Hiko would come home tonight, or if I'd ever see her, but I hoped that I could at least say I was sorry, say it in a way that was meaningful and not just the knee-jerk instinct that had come out of me before in so many ways. I didn't expect forgiveness, but I hoped that she would at least let me say the words.

I sat on the bed and looked at myself in the window. The clock chimed and I turned to look at it. By the time it struck its third and final chime, I had tears in my eyes. Beside the clock sat the plaster cast of my face. Without Hiko there I couldn't ask why she had it by her side of the bed. Without her there the closest I could get to her was the mask. It may have been my face, but it was made up of her. I think that's why I was so affected by it. It looked like me, but it felt like her.

I stepped to the table and reached out for the mask. Drops of blood fell onto the face, streaking along the eyes and nose. That's when I saw the glass in my arm. A beautifully narrow three-inch triangle of glass rose from my inner forearm like a shark's fin. Blood leaked, flowed along the glass, and with a steady drip fell to the floor. Fresh spots of blood at my feet, with a few back to where I had sat on the bed. Bloody handprints and streaked stains littered the bedspread. Back at the doorway drops of blood dotted the floor. They connected all the places I'd been. Some areas were tightly clustered with blood and other parts of the hallways and stairs had long gaps between splatters, making me think of constellations. The light switch was painted with bloody fingerprints and trails of blood fell along the wall beneath.

My hand still hung above the white plaster face. The chalk color turned red with blood that continued to fall from the glass. My blood dotted the mask, pooled and ran from the nose and eyes and streaked down the cheeks toward the base. Hiko had once asked me if I had bloodied her artwork and I had lied. Not anymore, I realized.

I left the room without touching the mask, the one thing I'd come to find, and I followed the drops of blood I'd left throughout the house. Again and again I found bloody handprints on walls and door frames, small clusters showing pauses. The hardwood floor's pattern sometimes hid the spots, sometimes showed it off. I looked for something other than just the recent blood, more drops underneath these fresh ones to show that I'd been in this house before, that I'd lived there. Underneath the blood, or maybe deeper in the wood there had to be some imprint I'd left behind, and not just here but out the door and down the street. Deeper in the ground or in the air surrounding those places I'd lived, where I'd performed or simply stood as I talked with Mal or Hiko or even Emilia or Darla, there had to be something of me there, something that would remain. I walked down the steps and saw only my newest bloodstains. I kept looking, and knew that I would probably never stop looking deeper, and deeper, for some sign of me.

At the front door gathered voices and flashing blue and red lights. A police car sat at the curb, Hiko beside it. One of two policemen consoled her, the other drew his gun when I emerged from her home. I stopped and raised my hands above my head.

I called out to Hiko, "It's me, Hiko." Her head snapped toward me. Her black glasses reflected the blue and red strobes of the car lights. She said something too soft for me to hear. The larger of the two policemen tried to pull her away from the building but she turned on him and said something else. Voices squawked from the police car radio. I kept my hands up. I raised them higher.

By the time Hiko explained that she knew me and would not press charges, the cops had noticed my cut. The glass kept getting caught on my clothes as my arm moved, and it alternately pulled partway out or pushed back in and I bled worse as a result.

The officers spoke to one another about my cut, and one of them suggested getting out their first-aid kit.

To the air between the cops Hiko said, "You have to take us to the hospital."

"We'll call you an ambulance, miss," said the smaller officer. The larger gave him a sharp look, then told us to get into the back of the car. From the trunk he pulled a med kit and loosely wrapped my arm.

"Does it hurt much?" he asked. I smiled and said that it did not and Hiko started to laugh. I knew she could hear my smile when I talked. I half believed she could hear it even when I didn't.

The police drove us up Seventh Avenue and headed toward Methodist Hospital. I watched Hiko, her head tilted to the side as if staring at the cop in front of her. "What are you doing here?" she asked.

"I wanted to apologize. For everything."

"You already did that."

"Did I?"

She didn't answer. I had, of course, or I had but hadn't meant it, or meant it but didn't know what I meant. My head began to swim.

The bandage around my arm turned red as it soaked up more blood. There were dark splatters across my lap and the seat. "I've done so many dumb—"

"You broke into my home to say sorry?"

"I couldn't wait for you to be home."

She laughed. "That doesn't make any sense." She stopped laughing suddenly. We were testing each other, feeling our way along the edges, trying to figure out the shape of what we were.

"My God, Hiko. I'm so sorry."

She didn't move, only held her hands on her lap and faced the back of the car seat ahead of her as the two policemen pretended not to listen.

We pulled up to the emergency room entrance. Hiko couldn't see, yet she insisted I lean on her for support. We stepped through the fluorescent, buzzing entrance. A room full of bored, ill, or crying visitors greeted us. A group of four men and two women, all in black turtleneck sweaters and jeans, stood around a woman alternating between tears and laughter. Their expressions rotated between support, concern, and disinterest. Two men stared at each other from across the waiting room, both with cell phones to their ears, possibly talking to each other. Around the island desk in the middle hovered three staff people in white coats, name tags perched on their lapels. The oldest of them, a woman with gray dreadlocks tightly tied at the back of her head, smiled as we approached and asked me to fill out paperwork. Somehow I skipped ahead of everyone else in the waiting room because a male orderly arrived shortly and ushered me to an exam room. He opened the door and we discovered a man in green scrubs on his hands and knees, wiping the floor with a wad of paper towels. The orderly turned to me with a confused grin.

"Lost control of a water bottle," the man wiping the floor said. He blushed a bit. The orderly left us there, shaking his head. I was unsure whether we should follow him or not. The man on the floor cleared water I couldn't really see and Hiko stood next to me, holding the door frame, her hand on my elbow.

She said, "How are you doing?"

I resisted an instinct that told me to say, *I'm okay*. Instead I told her how grateful I was that she was there. "I don't deserve your help."

Hiko said, "You may, or you may not. I haven't decided." She poked at my arm as she said this, letting me know it was as much the truth as it was a tease.

The man finished cleaning the floor and threw the towels into a bin. He stood, almost as tall as me, his face covered with exhaustion and three days of beard, and said, "Okay, sorry about that. What can I do for you?" At his neck hung an ID tag with large red letters: *MD*. He looked about nineteen years old.

Speechless for so long that Hiko reached for me, asked if I had passed out, I said, "You're the doctor?"

"Yep, that's me." He held up the ID. It could have been a high school yearbook photo. "So, what's up?"

"I'm sorry." I felt dizzy. "You were just cleaning the floor."

Hiko had missed that, of course. "He was cleaning what?"

The doctor turned to her. "And you are? Are you a spouse? Only spouses can be here."

I almost blurted out that she was my wife. Instead, Hiko calmly said, "Please, doctor. Please let me stay." She didn't press it as hard as she might have if she'd fully forgiven me, but her asking to stay felt like a small offering.

The doctor considered her a moment, semiprofessionally looking at her face, maybe only then realizing she was blind. "Yeah, sure, what the hell."

No one spoke while he examined me. As he prepared to remove the glass, I took Hiko's hand and said, "Can we—" I took a deep breath as I discovered I didn't know how to end that sentence.

Hiko nodded, removed her glasses. Her eyes fell on me, a happy accident. I saw my reflection in them, smiling at me. "Okay," she said. "We can talk. But first, let's just get this done."

The doctor prepared a suture kit. I looked at the tray, needles packed in a clear plastic case and individual sutures in a row in a folded cardboard backing. "After I remove this we'll have to close it up quickly and you'll probably have to go to surgery for more work. It doesn't seem too bad, but we may find it goes deeper than it looks." He pulled out a needle and a bottle of Novocain.

"I don't need that," I said.

"You sure? This is gonna hurt." The bags under his eyes made his eyes seem older than the rest of his face. I decided that maybe he wasn't so young after all.

"I'm sure."

He held the syringe and bottle of painkiller a moment, looking at the glass in my arm and then at me, uncertain what to do. He didn't know who I was. I wanted to warn him he might end up in a movie for this.

"You're sure?" He had trouble putting that syringe down.

"I don't need it."

He went to a cupboard and pulled out more gauze. As he did so, Hiko said, "Why did you break in? Why couldn't you wait?"

"I had to see you. I had to do something."

"Even if it was stupid," she added.

I concentrated on my arm. Betadine poured from elbow to wrist turned my arm a deep orange-brown. The glass poked up brightly, shining under the surgical light. I felt a tingle along the edge of the glass where it entered my arm.

"Stupid is better than nothing," I said.

She tilted her head toward me. "Maybe it is."

"The doctor agrees," the doctor said. "Now hold still." With a firm grip on either side of the three-inch triangle he pulled. The glass made a sucking sound similar to nails as they are removed, but deeper, more substantial. Hiko squeezed my other hand as she listened. Another mysterious tingle ran through the cut as the doctor pulled the glass free. Blood quickly pooled in the gap the glass left behind and spilled over, ran down my arm.

Hiko said, "May I have the glass?"

The doctor looked at her, then me, eyes asking if crazy ran in her family. I asked her why.

"I was thinking I might use it in a new piece."

I nodded. To the doctor I said, "She's an artist." He only raised his eyebrows in response, certain now that we were both insane. He brought out the needles and sutures to begin closing my arm.

The glass lay on the counter behind the doctor. It proved to be two inches longer than it had looked, the missing length having been in my arm. It rested on a pile of gauze, soaked in my blood. I asked Hiko, "What will you do with it?"

"I don't know. I'll let you know when I decide."

My attention pulled back to my arm as the doctor tugged the needle through the skin, reminding me of all the nails that had gone through me. But beneath the tugging there was another sensation, something hinting that it would get stronger. It grew—sharp, glaring, and persistent. Then the needle left my skin, pulling the suture behind, and the sensation left with it. I squeezed Hiko's hand with my free one as the doctor brought the second suture in.

"I can't believe you can't feel this," he said, and he pushed the needle through. Again, beneath the tug burned that other feeling, something I wanted to retreat from if it grew much larger, which it did. My arm twitched.

The doctor saw. "You sure you don't want something for the pain?"

I lost my breath for a moment, then smiled at him. "No. Nothing for the pain. Thanks."

He prepared the third suture and I lifted Hiko's hand up as if to kiss it, then realized I needed to move slowly, give her time and give myself time too. I watched the needle hang over my arm; the open wound tingled again, longer than before, and then the tip of the needle, the infinitely small point, came against my skin. In that moment before it punched through I had hope that with that one needle, or the next, or the next, I would hurt. I watched as it came so close to breaking the skin. Unable to wait any longer, I began to lift my arm, just barely, hoping that if I could only meet it halfway, I might find my lost sensation and my fear of pain and, in finding it, move beyond it for good.

SCHLOW CENTRE REGION LIBRARY
211 S. Allen Street
State College, PA 16801